Cy sat down and folded his arms. 'It's my dream. And I want to finish it, and, and . . . I'm going to dream up a few more happenings.' He concentrated really hard, and then looked up. 'I'd move if I were you,' he said. 'The whole of the Egyptian army is charging up behind you.'

'Pull the other one,' said the Dream Master. 'It's got camel bells on it.' He sat, resolute, arms still folded, but Cy noticed that his left eyebrow was twitching ever so slightly.

'Don't say I didn't warn you,' said Cy. And he added a few sound effects.

'*Very* impressive,' said the Dream Master sarcastically, leaping aside to avoid being trampled.

'Yes, *I* thought so,' said Cy, as he watched the chariots, horsemen, bowmen, and archers disappearing over a sand-dune. He was quite glad now that he had paid attention in class when Mrs Chalmers was describing the Ancient Egyptian armies of King Tutankhamun . . .

Have you ever woken up in the middle of a really good dream? Juat at the most exciting bit, when something sensational is about to happen? Supposing you could get back into your own dream . . .? Explore story structure with Cy and his Dream Master via the fast-paced and funny time-slip adventures written by award-winning author, Theresa Breslin.

**DREAM MASTER
DREAM MASTER NIGHTMARE
DREAM MASTER GLADIATOR
DREAM MASTER ARABIAN NIGHTS**

<u>www.theresabreslin.co.uk</u>

The DREAM MASTER

Theresa Breslin

Illustrated by David Wyatt

CORGI YEARLING BOOKS

THE DREAM MASTER
A CORGI YEARLING BOOK : 9780440863823

First published in Great Britain by Doubleday,
a division of Random House Children's Books

PRINTING HISTORY
Doubleday edition published 1999
Corgi Yearling edition published 1999

11 13 15 17 19 20 18 16 14 12

Corgi Yearling Books are published by Random House Children's Books,
61–63 Uxbridge Road, London W5 5SA,
a division of The Random House Group Ltd.

Addresses for Random House Group Ltd companies outside the UK
can be found at: www.randomhouse.co.uk
The Random House Group Ltd Reg. No. 954009.

Printed and bound in Great Britain by
Cox & Wyman Ltd, Reading, Berkshire.

The Random House Group Limited makes every effort to ensure that the
papers used in its books are made from trees that have been legally
sourced from well-managed and credibly certified forests. Our paper
procurement policy can be found at: www.randomhouse.co.uk/paper.htm.

Mixed Sources
Product group from well-managed
forests and other controlled sources
www.fsc.org Cert no. TT-COC-2139
© 1996 Forest Stewardship Council
FSC

A gift for Heva

Chapter 1

'Off with his head!'

The high priest of the mighty Pharaoh raised his hand and gave the signal to the executioner who stood awaiting his command.

Cy gasped as the death order was called out. He would have to act quickly if he was to save the life of his friend. The executioner stepped out from the shadow of the Great Pyramid and walked forward. As he raised his curved sword it caught the rays of the noonday sun, and for one single second everyone was blinded by the glare. Everyone

except Cy, who saw his chance and did not hesitate. He slapped his horse hard on its rump and galloped across the firm sand.

'Get ready!' he shouted. 'I'm coming!'

The young man who was kneeling on the ground looked up. Two terrified, wide brown eyes stared out from under a fringe of thick black hair. 'My friend!' he cried. 'I knew you'd come for me!' He stretched out his hands and began to scramble to his feet . . .

Behind him Cy heard a yell of fury, and he spurred on his horse. But below him the sand was changing, shifting under the horse's hooves, becoming deeper.

Cy reached out to the boy who was running towards him, but just as their fingers touched Cy's horse faltered, stumbling in the sand. Cy gripped the horse's mane with both hands but it was no use. As it reared and plunged he was thrown, and then he was rolling . . . rolling down and down, into a long, deep dune. The sand was everywhere, in his mouth, eyes, ears. He could hear his friend calling 'Help! Help!'

The sand around Cy was dissolving into dust. He lay sprawled out at the bottom of the slope, watching as the Egyptian desert began to drift away.

'Oh no!' Cy moaned. 'No!'

It always happened like this when he was having a good dream. He awoke at the very best part. Other times, when he had rotten dreams, he could never get out of them when he wanted to. Like the time he'd dreamt he'd needed the toilet, and wanted to go desperately, and then woke up *way* too late.

But not now, he thought bitterly. This time, just when it was getting interesting, and he'd been about to do something clever and brave, it was all disappearing. It wasn't fair! He snatched angrily at the dream as it floated off.

And – something snatched back.

From beyond the Dreamworld a force was pulling against him. Cy held on like fury.

'Let go!' a voice hissed in his ear.

'No way!' said Cy, grabbing now with both hands. 'This is *my* dream and I'm keeping it.'

'Correction. *I* am the Dream Master.'

'Who?' asked Cy. 'And,' he glanced around him, 'where, exactly, are you?'

'Right here, you ... you ... Earthbound Expectorant!'

Whatever was pulling against him suddenly let go, and Cy shot forward through the vapour right into his dream.

'Sixteen Stuttering Scorpions! Now look what you've done!'

Cy looked. He was back in his Egyptian dream, but it was not quite the same. For a start it was extremely thin, and the light kept alternating from bright to almost dusk. And his horse . . . his horse. He could almost, yet not quite, see it. Cy frowned, trying to recall what it had been like. It had been black, an Arab stallion. And, as Cy remembered, it shimmered into being.

'Oh,' he exclaimed, as he realized what was happening. He spoke aloud. 'When I think about something . . . it appears.'

'No,' said a voice behind him. 'No. No. No. No. No.'

Cy turned. There was a small dwarf sitting cross-legged on the sand, glaring at him. He had wrapped round him a cloak of black, dreamy silk.

'No. Negative. *Niet*,' said the dwarf. 'Your dream is over. Finished. *Kaput*. No more. *Finito*. Gone.' He held his cloak up. 'Look, you can almost see right through it. It's fading away.'

'No it isn't,' said Cy. He prodded at the sides of his dream, which seemed less filmy and fragile than a moment ago. 'It's going to last for ages.'

The dwarf stood up. 'You don't realize what

you've done, do you?' he spat. 'Dreams are supposed to be *inside* your head, Dunderhead. Not the other way about. You've gone and pulled yourself into *your own dream*. It's against all the rules.'

'What rules?' asked Cy. 'I didn't know there were rules.'

'There are *always* rules,' said the dwarf. He sat down again and folded his arms. 'It doesn't matter anyway. *I* am the Dream Master. Not you. What I say goes. And I say this dream is gone, so beat it.'

'No,' said Cy. He sat down and folded *his* arms. 'It's my dream. And I want to finish it, and, and . . . I'm going to dream up a few more happenings.' He concentrated really hard, and then looked up. 'I'd move if I were you,' he said. 'The whole of the Egyptian army is charging up behind you.'

'Pull the other one,' said the Dream Master. 'It's got camel bells on it.' He sat, resolute, arms still folded, but Cy noticed that his left eyebrow was twitching ever so slightly.

'Don't say I didn't warn you,' said Cy. And he added a few sound effects.

'*Very* impressive,' said the Dream Master sarcastically, leaping aside to avoid being trampled.

'Yes, *I* thought so,' said Cy, as he watched the chariots, horsemen, bowmen, and archers disappearing over a sand-dune. He was quite glad now that he had paid attention in class when Mrs Chalmers was describing the Ancient Egyptian armies of King Tutankhamun.

The Dream Master shook the sand from his hair. 'You really do have to wake up now,' he said. 'Listen.' Cy listened.

'Cy. Cy,' a voice called.

'That's my friend,' he told the Dream Master. 'I was just about to rescue him.'

'Listen again.'

Cy listened, and then groaned aloud. It was his mother's voice he heard, calling him to get up for school.

'You see?' said the dwarf. 'I had this planned perfectly. It was natural awakening. It all tied in with the dream. Your friend calling you becomes Mum. Wakey-wakey! No more Ancient Egypt. Mummies the word! Ha! Ha! She'll be thundering through that bedroom door in one shuddering second.' The Dream Master pointed out of the dream and laughed nastily.

Cy could see his bedroom as if through the wrong end of the telescope. 'It's not fair,' he said. 'I've got rights.'

'Ah . . .' The Dream Master stopped laughing.

12

'What do you know about your rights . . . exactly?'

'Well, I've got them, haven't I?' said Cy.

'Ummm,' said the dwarf. He looked around nervously. 'Ummm,' he said again. 'Under certain special circumstances a person can make contact with the same dream again. You *might* be able to come back and finish this one off.'

'So I would be like a Dream Master?' asked Cy.

'Don't talk ridiculous rubbish!' said the dwarf. 'All that's happened here is that you've flipped this dream over. I'll let you revisit it, but not just now.'

'When?' asked Cy.

'When it's possible.'

Cy could hear his mother's voice getting louder. 'How do I know I can trust you?'

'I'll leave you a sign.'

'What kind of a sign?'

'You'll know it when you see it. Now go!'

Cy went, diving for his duvet just as his bedroom door opened.

'Cy! Come *on*! You'll be late for school, and so will I, and my foreign exchange pupils are due this morning. Lauren's nearly finished breakfast, and she'll leave without you if you're not ready.'

Cy opened his eyes and looked up. Just for a

second he saw gently swaying palm trees, and then they changed to the spider's web which trailed across his *Star Wars* poster pinned to the ceiling. Such a pity, he thought.

'Do you ever dream the same dream twice?' he asked his mum as she hauled on his bedcovers.

'Not the good ones,' she said.

'That's what I thought,' said Cy.

'Cy, *please* hurry up. You know how crabby Lauren can be.'

Cy shook his head a couple of times, then swung his legs onto the floor and reached for his clothes.

'Lunch money!' His mother thrust some coins at him as he left the house. Cy, running to catch up with his older sister, shoved the change deep into his trouser pocket. Then he stopped still on the garden path. His stomach gave a queer lift and slowly, slowly, he pulled his hand back out and gazed at it.

There in his palm lay a little pile of sand. Not the coarse dark sand of the local beaches, but soft golden sand.

Sand such as you would find in the deserts of far Arabia.

Chapter 2

'Do you ever have strange dreams?' Cy asked Lauren as he caught up with her. 'Only when *you're* in them, Sproglet,' Lauren answered. She held one hand out in front of her, fingers splayed. 'What do you think of that colour of nail varnish?'

Cy's brain quickly registered two points.

a) His older sister had asked him for his opinion about something, and,

b) She had called him 'Sproglet'.

These were favourable omens. She must be in a

reasonably good mood, Cy thought. Normally Lauren paid him less attention than the weather report. Occasionally when she had no other option *but* to talk to him, she would get his attention by snapping her fingers, or by flicking his ear. She would also call him by her own specially created names, which ranged from semi-friendly to downright rude, depending on how she felt. He knew that if she had just now, called him Beast, Man-Cub, or Tiny Turd, then there would have been no point in continuing the conversation. Occasionally he was Cyberman, which meant that she was *almost* on speaking terms with him. But this morning she had used Sproglet. Sproglet was good. It meant that she was prepared to accept that, for the time being at any rate, he was at the same stage of evolutionary development as herself. Walking upright, and able to communicate verbally.

'It's called Screaming Sapphire,' she told him, flashing her fingertips under his nose.

Cy regarded the hideous bright blue nails offered for his inspection. He had been told that lying was wrong but, hey ... so was hurting the feelings of another living creature. And if the creature was his sister, whose rages were spectacular and often directed at him, well lying seemed the lesser evil.

'Brilliant,' Cy said, thinking that, technically, it *was* actually true. 'I had a weird dream, last night,' he went on. 'And when I woke up . . .' He paused.

'Yeah,' said Lauren, 'that's the annoying thing about dreams. Either something horrible is happening and you want it to finish, and it won't. Or else you wake up too early . . . Like the other night? I dreamt I was with Cartwheel and Baz at this tremendous gig. The warm-up group had gone off, BearBoyz had just come on, and the lead singer, Declan, you know him, don't you? He's the one with the really cute fringe, cut to just above his eyes . . . and he . . .'

'No.' Cy cut in immediately. He would never get to speak if she started wittering on about any of the new Boy Bands. She wouldn't stop until they had reached school, infinity and beyond. She might never stop. She and her two friends could go on for *days* about any or all of the Boy Bands. He knew this for a fact. Because one time, when they had been having a sleepover at his house, he had listened outside Lauren's bedroom door, practically all night to see if they had any good secrets. And all they had talked about for *hours* and

17

hours was Declan's fringe, and whether he looked better with his hair swept back, which showed off his high forehead, or flicked down which emphasized his eyes. 'No,' said Cy again. 'Not like that. This morning I woke up actually *inside* my dream.'

Lauren looked at him. 'Then you weren't awake,' she said. 'You were still asleep. You just *thought* you were awake. That happens. Sometimes Mum calls me. I get up and get dressed, and then she comes in and I'm still in bed. It's just that I've *dreamt* that I've done something I needed to do, or should be doing.'

'No, I've had that too,' Cy said. 'This was different, completely different. When I woke up the dream was drifting away. I felt it fading, sort of saw wisps of it in my room. It was at a really exciting bit, and I was so frustrated at waking up that I grabbed at it and pulled it back. And then . . . and then . . . I fell *into the dream*. The dream wasn't in me, not inside my head in the normal way, like it's supposed to happen. I was inside the dream . . . And because of this I was in control, so . . . I could do what I wanted to.'

Lauren had stopped to listen. She peered at Cy closely. 'You're not doing anything stupid,' she said, 'like smoking funny cigarettes?'

'No!' said Cy in exasperation. 'Just listen, will you? It really happened. Honestly. There was this character there, like a small dwarf. He told me he was a Dream Master. He kept trying to get me to leave, and go out of the dream, and when I wouldn't, he got angry. That's when I realized that in this case, I had some kind of control that you don't usually have in dreams.'

'So, what happened?' asked Lauren.

'Well, actually . . . I woke up. I think.'

'Aw, for heaven's sakes!' said Lauren. 'That's pathetic! You had me going there for a minute.' She punched her brother's arm. 'Good story though. You might be able to use it in class. Keep it in mind, 'cos you know how useless you are at writing.'

'No, I'm not,' said Cy at once. 'Grampa says I've a good imagination.'

'Yeah, you can certainly make things up,' agreed Lauren. 'I meant the actual pen on the paper bit. So that other people can read it. Except in your case they can't. Squirrelly Squiggle hasn't a look in.'

'Well,' said Cy stubbornly, 'what I told you a minute ago wasn't a story. It happened like I said.'

'Of course it did,' said Lauren soothingly. She had just caught sight of her friends on the

19

pavement ahead and was no longer interested. 'Boys are weird,' he heard her tell her friends as she caught up with them. 'Seriously weird.'

'There are *some* exceptions,' giggled Cathy, the tallest of the group, whom they called Cartwheel. She opened her rucksack and pulled out a magazine.

'Get it?' said Barbara known as Baz. She nudged Lauren. 'Get it? Exceptions . . . X-Septyons!!!!!'

'Look!' Cartwheel had opened the magazine at the centre spread. She showed them the colour photograph of four youths. 'The X-Septyons!'

'Wow!' said Lauren. 'Can I have that for my bedroom wall?'

'Dream on!' said Cartwheel.

Dream on, thought Cy as the girls went off through the gates of the High School, and he wandered further down the road to his own school. He wished he could. He stuck his hand in his pocket and felt again the gritty grains of sand. Was this the sign the Dream Master had said he would leave?

Chapter 3

y slowed down as he walked towards his school. Crossing to the playground in the morning required forward thinking.

'Strategic planning,' Cy's Grampa often said, 'always pays off.'

Grampa had been one of General Montgomery's desert rats in the Western Desert during the Second World War, and Monty had often stopped by his tent looking for advice. 'I told him then,' said Grampa, 'as I'm telling you now, Cy, strategic planning is the key to survival.'

Cy sauntered casually over to the school crossing patrol. 'Activate Alien Alert,' he murmured as he bent down and fiddled with the strap on his trainers.

'Roger, wilco,' responded Mrs Turner from behind her STOP: CHILDREN CROSSING sign. 'Alien Alert activated.' She narrowed her eyes and swivelled round through 180 degrees. 'Bandits at six o'clock,' she said.

Cy lifted his head a little. There was a group of kids waiting to cross. He checked them out. All clear. And then he saw two of his classmates, Eddie and Chloe, coming out of the newspaper shop along the street ... the Mean Machines ... always on the lookout for someone to noise up. Cy quickly got to his feet.

Mrs Turner had covered her mouth with her hand. 'Aliens sighted,' she said. 'Awaiting instructions, Squadron Leader.'

Cy stared down the road. Eddie and Chloe had begun to walk up towards the crossing patrol. 'Evasive action,' he whispered.

'Excellent idea,' said Mrs Turner. Holding up her pole, she stepped into the road and the traffic screeched to a halt. 'Fast as you can,' she instructed Cy.

As he raced past Cy glanced back and saw Eddie and Chloe hurry to cross over. He heard Mrs Turner yell at them. 'Stop! Don't either of you move until I come back to take you across the road. After all,' she continued in a loud voice, 'we can't have little boys and girls crossing a busy road on their own.'

Cy grinned. Mrs Turner was a mate of Grampa's and she would delay those two for as long as she could on the other side. Cy kept a watchful eye as he entered the playground. Eddie and Chloe weren't the only aliens that he had to be wary of, but they were the worst, and with them held up for a bit he felt a lot easier as he pushed open the double swing doors.

It was always better inside school. The janitor and teachers were very strict about people being picked on and made a point of talking to each pupil they met in the corridors. The new head had put up BE BULLYPROOF posters all over the corridors with a list of DOs and DON'Ts, although Eddie and Chloe were good at finding some sly way to annoy their victims and look innocent at the same time. When things were bad last term, Cy's mum had sometimes waited with him until his bell rang before going on to the school on the other side of town where she taught foreign languages. Occasionally she had made Lauren accompany him all the way to school. That had been hell. Cy would almost rather have faced the bullies. His sister, annoyed at having to miss time with her friends, insisted on waiting with him until the bell rang. Then she would plant a huge smacky kiss on his cheek, leaving a lipstick trail, and coo 'Bye-byee, little bruvver' so loudly that Eddie and Chloe and the rest of the nasties would snigger and shout 'Bye-byeee' to each other until a teacher came out and told them to stop.

'There are bullies everywhere,' Cy's Grampa said. 'You think Eddie and his team are one-offs. They ain't.' He tapped Cy on the head. 'Out-think them, son. The way I had to at the club.'

Grampa had told Cy that for a while every Wednesday at the Old Folks Club Mrs Nirijandi always took the best set of dominoes to play with her friends, and Grampa had to make do with the set with the faded dots and pieces missing. Once, when Grampa had got there first, she had actually snatched the new box right out of his hand! And he had been too much of a gentleman to grab it back.

'But I out-thunk her son,' Grampa told Cy. One week he had waited behind and swapped the sets over, putting the old dominoes into the new box. The following week Mrs Nirijandi got a very nasty shock when she opened her box, and after that she didn't know which set to pick.

'There's always bad guys,' said Cy's Grampa. 'Fortunately, there's also always good guys. Just you make sure you've got yourself sorted as to which team *you're* in.'

Cy shouldered his rucksack and went into the school assembly hall. It was nearly the end of term, and Cy's class were decorating the walls with a frieze on the Ancient Egyptians. He went to the section he was doing, the picture-writing on the great columns which held up the Pharaoh's hypostyle hall.

Cy took a felt-tip from his schoolbag and carefully outlined a red oval mouth shape on one of the long pillars. He had been amazed that Mrs Chalmers had let him do the hieroglyphs.

'Cy's not good at writing,' Chloe had sneered, when the teacher was discussing who should do what.

'This is special writing,' Mrs Chalmers had replied smartly. 'I'm sure Cy will be as good at it as any Ancient Egyptian.'

Cy drew a small bird below his mouth shape. It

didn't matter if these were a bit squint. The Egyptians didn't know about ruled jotters, although they did draw little oblong boxes round special names. Cy hated writing in class. He was so clumsy, his wrist and fingers didn't seem to be in tune with his brain. And especially he hated doing it when sitting opposite Chloe, whose tidy letters sat so smugly on the page. It was such an effort for him to keep every single character straight, and his hand got so tired. He was looking forward to the age of telepathic communication which would take all that bother away. Only, the trouble with telepathy was that it would work both ways. So, if he could read the minds of others, then they could read his. Cy recalled his conversation earlier with Lauren, and what he had been really thinking about her nail varnish. Perhaps not yet.

Cy looked at his watch. He might manage another symbol before the bell went. It must have been even worse learning letters in Egyptian times. There were hundreds of different ones! He glanced along the wall to the figure of a boy being taught by a scribe. It was the first time Cy had seen this bit, as Mrs Chalmers had only begun outlining the scene yesterday. She must have stayed behind after school to finish painting the details. The boy had his script brush in his hand and broken pieces of pottery and stones lay around him in the sand.

Cy turned back to his drawing and then stopped, his felt-tip pen halfway to the wall. Slowly he stepped back from the frieze and looked again at the writing master and his pupil. Cy stared hard at the face of the boy scribe.

From underneath a fringe of thick black hair two familiar wide brown eyes stared back.

Chapter 4

Cy's own eyes opened wide. It couldn't be ... How was it possible that the boy in his dream last night was on the school's Egyptian frieze?

'Do you like him?'

Cy jumped. Mrs Chalmers was standing behind him.

'I'm not completely happy with my young scribe,' she said. 'It took me ages to do the face, and it's still not right. He looks a bit odd ...' She laughed. 'Almost as though he's scared of something.'

'He is,' said Cy. 'He's going to be executed.'

'What?' Mrs Chalmers looked at Cy's worried face and then shook her head. 'What an imagination you have, Cy. It's only a picture,' she said, laughing again.

'Only a picture.' Mrs Chalmers' words stayed in Cy's head all through the school day. Wasn't that what dreams were? Pictures inside your head. But dreams were usually mixed up memories of previous events. In this case he had dreamt about the boy *before* Mrs Chalmers had drawn him.

Later that morning, Cy leafed through the Egyptian resource materials in the classroom project corner. Perhaps he had seen the boy somewhere here? Eventually, in one of the books, Cy found a drawing which was quite similar. An Egyptian priest stood studying a roll of papyrus, while his boy pupil knelt at his feet, reed paintbrush in hand, palette and inks by his side. Except, this boy did not stare out at the world with a frightened expression on his face. His head was bent, his eyes shaded by his heavy fringe of hair.

'That's the picture I copied for our wall frieze,' said Mrs Chalmers, leaning over Cy's shoulder. 'Perhaps I should have made my scribe have his head bowed too.'

'No,' said Cy. 'I like seeing his eyes. It's more . . . more lifelike. What is he wearing round his neck?' Cy pointed to the pendant which hung at the boy's throat.

'It is an ankh, probably made from silver,' said Mrs Chalmers. '*Ankh* meant "mirror" in Ancient Egypt. The shape had a particular significance. It was linked to your spirit or your soul. People would wear them to keep themselves safe from harm. It appears in many of the ancient paintings and papyruses.' Mrs Chalmers flicked through the book until she found an illustration. 'This shows the Journey to the Afterlife when each human being is called to account for their deeds. Here are the scales where the jackal-headed god Anubis is weighing the person's heart against the Feather of Truth. Thoth, the god of wisdom, is writing a record of the person in his book, while the other gods are acting as judges. They are seated above the scales, and the person awaiting judgement is holding an ankh. And here,' she showed Cy some picture-writing, 'when it is drawn as a hieroglyph, the ankh was a word on its own. It symbolized life.'

'Life,' Cy repeated. He turned the page back to

the boy scribe, and traced the outline of the ankh with his finger. He looked up at Mrs Chalmers. 'Did you give your boy an ankh?'

'No,' said Mrs Chalmers. 'No, I didn't actually.'

At break-time, as he sat in the classroom eating his packed lunch, Cy took the silver paper from his chocolate biscuit wrapper and carefully twisted the foil into an ankh shape. He fashioned one long stick about a quarter the size of a straw and put a crossed spar one third of the way down the length. Then he added another piece to the top and pulled it up and round into an elongated circle. In the craft cupboard he found a piece of black cord and threaded it through the loop at the top. Then he held it up to inspect it. It looked quite authentic. Cy spun the amulet round and round, and watched as the twisted cord slowly unravelled. The foil glittered in the light. I should wear it, thought Cy. It might protect me from the Mean Machines.

Suddenly, with his free hand Cy reached out and stopped the spinning ankh. He stared at it for a moment or two and then he got up, thrust it in his pocket, and hurried along the corridor. The assembly hall was empty, the door creaked in the quietness as Cy slipped in. He went to where Mrs Chalmers' boy scribe sat patiently on the dusty sand, with one hand holding the russet-tipped brush firmly in his fingers.

'Look,' whispered Cy. 'Here is an ankh. If you are in trouble it should help to keep you safe.' And using some Blu-Tack Cy fastened the silver amulet round the neck of the boy scribe.

Later Cy wished he had kept it for himself.

After lunch Mrs Chalmers got the whole class working hard on the props for their Egyptian play. 'We'll leave Tutankhamun's mask until later,' she said. 'I want to use plaster and make it very special. Today I would like to finish the Great Pyramid. Everyone to their tasks please.'

Mrs Chalmers had given out sheets of brown paper, which was meant to resemble papyrus, and Cy was copying out some hieroglyphs and figures. He mixed up some paints in jars and began carefully to paint the outlines.

Eddie and Chloe were working nearby, tacking pieces of cardboard onto a wooden frame to make the base of the Great Pyramid, while Vicky, Basra and Innis were making a triangular cap to sit on top.

'Cy,' Vicky called out, 'could you help us with this?'

Cy left his painting and went to help Vicky hold the four triangular pieces tightly in place as Innis and Basra glued the pieces together. When it was finished they all stood back to admire it.

'It looks great,' said Cy.

'We've still to mark out the lines,' said Basra. 'We had to wait until it was glued otherwise the lines might not have joined up properly.'

Cy left them to it and went back to his own work at the counter under the window. As he walked past Eddie and Chloe they sniggered loudly.

' "C" for Cy, "C" for clumsy,' tittered Eddie.

Cy looked down at his painting. Two of the paint jars had been tipped over and the coloured liquid was spilling out across the paper.

'Oh,' said Cy. 'Oh no!'

'Oh dear, Cy,' said Mrs Chalmers, 'not again!'

'But Miss—'

'Never mind,' interrupted Mrs Chalmers in a brisk voice. 'Just clear it up as best you can.'

She gave a little shake of her head as she moved away. Cy felt hot tears of shame start behind his eyelids and he blinked quickly. It wasn't fair. He knew it wasn't his fault this time. He was sure it had been Eddie and Chloe, but you couldn't tell tales. And you could never get your own back. Now no-one was even allowed to *say* anything to them. Mrs Chalmers had heard someone shouting 'Mean Machines' in the playground one day and had immediately forbidden all name calling, saying she would send anyone she heard using rude names straight to the Head.

Cy looked at the mess. As usual, panic was slowing him down. He couldn't think what to do. He gazed helplessly at the spreading pool of paint.

Vicky raised her head from her table and gasped. 'Oh, Cy!' She grabbed some paper tissues, ran over, and quickly laid them flat across the pool of paint. 'There, that'll sop it up.' She grinned at Cy. 'I knock over the milk at home practically every day. That's how I know how to sort it quick.'

Cy gave her a grateful look. 'I think it was those two,' he whispered. He nodded at Eddie and Chloe, who were now industriously hammering away and chatting together.

'The Mean Machines?' Vicky mouthed the words out.

Cy nodded.

'Never mind,' said Vicky. 'One day, someone will fix them. Someone will fix them real good.'

After school Grampa was in his usual place, leaning on the school gate.

'Do you believe in dreams?' Cy asked him at
once.

Grampa repeated the question. 'Do I believe in
dreams?' He thought for a moment. 'Yes,' he said.
'I think I do. In fact, there are days when I believe
in nothing else.'

That was one of the things Cy liked about
Grampa. He didn't hedge around when asked a
question. Most adult answers to difficult questions
were qualified by phrases such as: 'Under certain
circumstances . . .' Or else they added bits on: 'But
what you've got to remember is . . .' or they even
managed to bring in boring political messages by
saying things like: 'However, under the present
government . . .' As if anyone *cared*.

Cy told Grampa all about his strange dream of
last night as they walked to his house.

'I guess I could go along with Time being a con-
cept,' said Grampa as he took out his key and
opened his front door. 'You know what Einstein
said, "Imagination is everything".' Grampa
knocked the top of Cy's head very gently. 'And
you've certainly got dollops of that in there.'

'Yeah,' said Cy gloomily. 'But a lot of crossed wires as well. Nothing co-ordinates. And the harder I try, the worse it gets.'

Grampa laughed. 'Well, don't try so hard. I'm serious,' he added as Cy made a face. 'Einstein never passed a single maths exam at school.'

As Grampa got down juice and biscuits from a cupboard, Cy took the sand from his pocket and put it on the kitchen table.

Grampa raised one eyebrow. 'Now that *is* very strange,' he said softly as he let the grains trickle through his long, strong fingers. 'The last time I felt sand like that I was in the Western Desert.' He found an empty matchbox and carefully scooped it inside. 'You must tell me tomorrow if you have that dream again tonight.'

But it wasn't until a few nights later that the Dream Master came again.

Cy was lying on his bed waiting for sleep and half watching the ancient spider's web which trailed across the *Star Wars* poster on his ceiling. He studied the tendrils carefully, remembering that he had once seen them as palm trees. Probably because of the glossy green leaves and the brown coconuts. Cy blinked. Somehow he wasn't at all taken aback to see that there were now coconuts growing on the spider's web on his bedroom ceiling. He twisted round on his bed to get a better look at them.

'You'll go squint-eyed if you stare like that.'

Cy turned his head. Sitting cross-legged on the pillow beside him was the Dream Master.

Chapter 5

'Where have you been?' asked Cy.

'Where have *I* been?' said the dwarf.

'Hanging around waiting for you, mate. You lead such lives in this time level. Frantic isn't the word. I've been trying to get a word in edgewise for aeons.'

'Several days actually,' said Cy.

'Days?' repeated the dwarf. 'Oh I see. You mean the "sun-up, sun-down" thing. Time doesn't work like that.'

'How does it work, then?' asked Cy.

'It doesn't *work* at all,' said the dwarf. 'It just *is*. Look, never mind,' he went on quickly, 'you wouldn't understand.'

'Yes I would.'

Cy knew that adults often said 'you wouldn't understand' when they couldn't be bothered to go into details. He quoted his Grampa: 'Understanding relies on things being properly explained.'

The Dream Master gave him a strange look. 'You know, Einstein said the exact same thing to me last time I saw him.'

'You met Einstein!'

'We were playing chess,' said the dwarf. 'I was winning, if you must know,' he added smugly.

'You beat Einstein at chess!' said Cy.

'Well,' said the dwarf. 'It was *my* dream. Anyway, let's get on. I came back because I made a promise, but I have to tell you that I've got a bad feeling about that Ancient Egyptian dream. I think you'd be much better off in a new one which I can create for you.' He opened up a laptop which had just materialized on his knees. 'Now let me see what's on for tonight . . .' He fiddled with the keyboard. 'I could do you a rather thrilling adventure with Alexander the Great.'

39

'No thanks,' said Cy.

'Alien invaders?' the dwarf suggested. 'There's a good programme called "Beat the Bullies". You could destroy the Mean Machines.'

Cy thought for a moment. 'No. Thanks all the same.'

The dwarf frowned at his screen. 'How about leading Hannibal across the Alps? No? Mmm? Fight at Waterloo? Hold on while I check who's winning at present. Oh no, that's too awful. Ummm . . . meet Queen Victoria? Wait! I know. Let's take part in some "Gruesome Gladiator Games" . . . a visit to Ancient Rome.'

'Ancient *Egypt*,' said Cy firmly.

The dwarf was getting impatient. 'Starring role in *Coronation Street*? Three episodes.'

Cy shook his head.

'Present *Blue Peter*?' said the dwarf.

'I've got a life,' said Cy.

'A *Star Wars* spectacular,' said the dwarf. 'And that's my final offer.'

Cy hesitated. 'No,' he said at last.

'What!' cried the dwarf. 'I know people who would *kill* for that. Are you actually telling me that you do *not* want to be a Jedi knight?'

'Not at the moment,' said Cy.

'Princess Leia would be *tremendously* grateful,' coaxed the dwarf. He glanced upwards. Cy followed his gaze. Princess Leia smiled down from his bedroom ceiling. Cy heard the tapping of the Dream Master's keyboard. The princess lifted her laser gun and one of her coiled plaits tumbled across her shoulder. With an imperious gesture she dismissed Han Solo and Luke Skywalker. Her huge dark eyes sent a plea across the galaxies.

'Help me, Obi-Cy Kenobi,' she called. 'You're my only hope—'

'Don't do that,' said Cy sharply.

The dwarf snapped his laptop closed. 'I could make you appear as one of the BearBoyz,' he said nastily.

Cy shuddered. 'Look,' he said. 'I want to go back to Ancient Egypt.' He paused. 'I *have* to go back.'

The Dream Master gave Cy a searching look from beneath bushy eyebrows. 'Why did you say "*have* to"?'

'I'm not sure,' said Cy. He thought about the boy in the wall frieze who had the same haunting eyes as the boy he had seen in his dream. 'I think there is something there that I must sort out.'

'Oh-oh,' said the dwarf. 'The last time I got into this kind of bother was with a fellow by the name of Rip van Winkle. He *completely* exhausted me. This sounds like trouble.'

'Trouble?'

'Yes. Trouble. Twenty types of trouble – double-mixed,' said the dwarf. 'You shouldn't be able to *sort out* anything in a dream. Humans don't have the power to control their dreams.'

'But this *is* my dream,' Cy complained. 'You said it was different.'

'Exactly,' said the dwarf. 'Which means I have to let you be in charge.'

'I *shall* be a Dream Master like you!' said Cy.

The Dream Master laughed a scornful laugh. 'Absolutely absurd! It would take a particular powerful force for you to ever get anywhere near to *my* level. But,' he hesitated, 'in this one instance, yes, you will have a sort of mastery over your dream.'

'Well, let's go!' said Cy.

'You have no experience,' said the Dream Master. 'It could be tricky.'

'So?' said Cy.

'If something goes wrong . . .'

'But dreams always go wrong,' Cy protested. 'Things happen all over the place.'

'How dare you!' said the dwarf. 'It requires

42

tremendous skill being a Dream Master. Your dreams may seem a trifle . . . er . . . disconnected at times but that is due to the peculiar way human minds function.'

'Well, my dream will be perfectly logical,' said Cy.

'Oh *really*.' The dwarf snorted. 'Just remember, at all times you must do exactly as I tell you.'

'Of course I will,' said Cy.

'Immediately I say it?'

'Instantly.'

'Promise?'

'Promise.'

'It's the only way that I can be sure that nothing will go wrong,' said the dwarf.

'Nothing will go wrong,' said Cy, uncrossing his fingers behind his back.

'Well, let's find out, shall we?' The Dream Master stood up. 'Take hold of a corner of my cloak, and <u>do not let go</u>.'

Cy rubbed his eyes. The dwarf was becoming smaller and smaller on his pillow, yet the Dream Master's cloak was growing. It billowed out like a great wave and enveloped Cy completely. The silky material was like black wind. Wind and water rushing past his face, fanning his hair, streaming out beside him and through him. Now it was racing ahead of him through a sky of spinning stars. Time itself moved, flowing towards him and then, changing direction, it began to accelerate away. Suddenly Cy remembered the dwarf's instruction. He leapt forward and, with a desperate grab, he clutched onto the tail-end of the Dream Master's cloak.

Chapter 6

Now the rushing motion was in Cy's head. His mind and emotions were dragged into a whirling river of thought. Then, quite suddenly, it stopped. Cy teetered. Black abyss all around. The silence was terrifying. Cy opened his mouth to speak and found that he couldn't. He tried to reach out with his hands and found he was unable to. He was unable to move, unable to think.

Round him a current still flowed but less strongly. And, as it slowed even more, he was

aware that the Dream Master was there.

'Listen,' the dwarf spoke urgently, 'the dream-time has a certain length, and you cannot change that. When it's time to leave ... you leave. *Capisce?*'

Cy nodded. He was beginning to regain a hold on his own reality.

'It must be absolutely understood,' said the dwarf, 'that when the dream goes, so do you. Although I don't know when that will be exactly.'

'In the books I read, it was always on the stroke of midnight,' Cy suggested helpfully.

The dwarf rolled his eyes. 'Great Giza,' he said. 'He thinks he's Cinderella.'

The flowing current had now stopped completely. Cy looked about. They appeared to be in a long stone corridor. A long, dark, stone corridor.

'Right,' said the dwarf. 'This should be Ancient Egypt, roughly at the same point where you left off.'

'We should be in the desert, then,' said Cy.

'And we're not, are we?' said the dwarf. He chewed his lip. 'I think we're further on.'

'Further on ... where?' asked Cy.

'Well, it's obvious, isn't it?' said the dwarf, glancing about anxiously.

Cy peered around. 'I can't see anything.'

'Open your eyes, why don't you?'

Cy put his hand to his face and touched his eyes. 'They *are* open,' he said. 'I *hate* dreams like this. I need some help here.'

'Do I have to do absolutely everything for you?' snapped the dwarf.

'A suggestion would be helpful,' Cy snapped back.

'Try saying "Let there be light", why don't you?'

Cy tried to imagine an electric light. He thought of a fluorescent tube. A long column, glowing bluish-white, appeared in his hand. 'This had better not be Obi-wan Kenobi's light-sabre,' said Cy.

The beam flickered and disappeared. A torch would be more useful, thought Cy. There was a clunk as something solid landed at his feet.

'Ah,' said Cy. He picked it up and clicked the switch. Nothing happened.

'Batteries not included,' sniggered a voice in his ear.

'*With* batteries,' Cy said aloud. A beam of light spread out before them. 'Omigosh!' said Cy. Two paces directly in front of him was a pit. 'I could have fallen in there,' he said.

'Yeah,' said the dwarf nastily.

'I think I want a rope,' said Cy.

'How do you know there aren't snakes in there?' asked the dwarf.

'Because . . .' Cy hesitated. Then he laughed. 'Because I didn't think there would be.'

The dwarf made a hissing noise. 'Are you sure? You've thought of them now though, haven't you? So they might be down there waiting for you.' And he chuckled.

'Don't be so horrible,' said Cy. He shone the torch ahead of him. 'I don't need a rope, anyway. I've decided that there are stairs leading down to a large room. Let's go.'

Cy touched the walls on either side as he led the way down the long staircase.

'Are we in a pyramid?' he asked. 'Or somewhere in the Valley of the Kings?'

'You tell me,' said the dwarf.

Cy lifted his torch and shone it around the room they had just entered. The walls were covered in bright paintings with row upon row of hiero-glyphics in vertical lines. Scenes of families at work in the fields, bakers making bread and a potter working at his wheel made a frieze around the sides of the room. Four great statues guarded the entrance to another chamber.

Cy turned to the dwarf. 'Should I go on?'

The Dream Master shrugged. 'Do you want to?'

Cy nodded. He pointed ahead. 'I want to know what's in there.'

The dwarf's eyes narrowed. 'But you should *know* what's in there. You are dreaming this up as you go along . . . aren't you?'

Cy looked away quickly. 'Umm . . .' he said, and his heart gave a quick flip. Perhaps he still had it in his mind that they had been making the Great Pyramid in class today, and that was why they were here . . . in some kind of burial chamber. But truthfully, he knew that he hadn't actually dreamt this up. It had just happened on its own. Also, things seemed to be happening incredibly quickly, at the very instant he thought about them. In fact . . . almost *faster* than he was thinking them.

The dwarf pulled at Cy's sleeve. 'You *are* dreaming this, aren't you? I mean, you haven't lost control of the dream, or anything?'

'Of course not.' Cy shook himself free and walked on. 'Omigosh,' he said as he entered the next room.

They were now in a burial antechamber, which was crammed full of everything that might be of use in a long Afterlife. There were urns and jugs of gold and beaten brass, ebony and cedarwood statues, many pieces of furniture, food and drink, amulets, necklaces, jewellery and precious stones. Every centimetre of the walls and roof had been painted upon. Figures, dancing, sitting and standing glowed vibrantly down at them.

'This must be a Pharaoh's tomb,' said Cy as he wandered around, picking up objects to look at them and replacing them carefully. There were little wooden statues covered with beaten gold, heavy armbands studded with glass beads and precious stones, boxes with intricate inlays, and some small model soldiers. An alabaster jar gleamed softly, the figures on the side silhouetted in the light. In one corner stood a wooden mummy case. In another was a throne-like chair with a leopard's head on each arm and four paws for feet.

A decorated chest showed the Pharaoh with his wife. Cy stared harder. Just for the briefest flicker Cy had thought that the Pharaoh had looked a bit like his dad. He looked again at the Pharaoh's wife. Tall ostrich feathers rose proudly from her head-dress, and immediately above was the shape of the long cross with the loop at the top. The ankh. Eternal life. The magical symbol of the life of the soul . . . Cy rubbed the back of his neck. He had an odd feeling growing inside . . . as if there was someone else close by. It must be the drawings, Cy told himself. He was surrounded by them. Scenes from everyday life, people working in the fields, hunting, fishing, and trapping birds with nets. The hieroglyphics on the wall seemed to resonate with colour. The clothes on the painted figures glistened white, their kohl-ringed eyes gazed out at him. Cy shivered. Lauren was right. He had too much imagination.

But the feeling of being watched was over-powering. Was it the sign-writing which was making him so uncomfortable? The little pictures of the birds and animals with their bright eyes. Or the larger statues, some of which had glass eyes which caused them to regard you with an eerie, lifelike look? Cy took a firm grip of his thoughts and tried to concentrate.

The prickly sensation still didn't go away. He paused to look at some papyrus scrolls and then, on the outer rim of his hearing he heard a soft noise.

Cy froze. He hadn't imagined *that*, had he? Not intentionally . . . but in a way he had, because nothing could exist in this dream without him thinking about it, even if only for a microsecond. Could it?

Cy lifted his head and listened. There it was again . . . a soft creaking noise, and then, suddenly, he was aware of a movement. He whirled round. The noise was coming from inside the wooden mummy case standing upright in the corner.

Chapter 7

Cy stared at the half-open mummy case. The dwarf smirked. 'Explain this one, oh Great Master-of-the-Mind who said, "My dream will be perfectly logical."'

'It's just a draught of air,' Cy said.

'Right inside the middle of a tomb?' said the dwarf. 'I don't think so.'

'Umm . . . we've been walking about and that's caused some vibration, and . . . and dislodged some stones,' explained Cy.

'Blithering Blethers!'

Cy took a couple of steps forward. 'Well, let's find out what's inside,' he said.

'Yes, do let's,' said the dwarf. 'I'm right behind you . . . a long way behind,' he added under his breath.

Cy gripped the edge of the partly open mummy case and dragging at it, widened the gap. Then he looked inside.

'Oh!' he stepped back quickly.

'Ouch!' said the dwarf and rubbed his nose. 'What is it?'

The body of a young man was propped up inside, hands crossed over his chest. He looks so peaceful, Cy thought.

An ankh amulet hung round its neck. As Cy watched, the knot on the leather cord at the front came loose and it fell with a soft chink at his feet. He picked it up and studied it more closely. It was similar to the one he had shaped out of foil, except that this one was real silver. A leather lace was threaded through the top loop.

'This is what caused the noise,' said Cy. 'The leather knot was coming undone. It's very new and stiff and doesn't bend properly.'

'Hmmph!' said the dwarf.

Cy looped the cord round his wrist, and then he

looked again at the face of the young man. 'Oh, no!' he said.

'What now?'

'It's the boy,' said Cy. 'The boy in my first dream. The one I tried to rescue . . .' Cy felt sick at heart as he gazed at the young man's face, waxy pale, eyes closed in death. 'I came back too late,' he said sadly.

The dwarf peered round from behind Cy. 'He's giving me the creeps,' he said. 'Close over the door.'

Cy looked at the boy for a moment or two longer, and then he raised his hands to close the wooden lid. As a last farewell he stretched out his hand and touched the boy's face. The skin under his fingers was warm.

Cy cried out and leapt backwards.

'Ouch! Ouch! Ouch!' yelled the dwarf, hopping about and trying to hold his toes and nose at the same time. 'Piffling Pyramids! What in the name of Royal Rameses are you playing at?'

'Shhh,' hissed Cy. 'Don't make a noise. I think he's still alive.'

'Don't be silly.' The dwarf spoke very quietly but fiercely. 'You cannot *possibly* create life.'

'I didn't,' whispered Cy.

'Why are we whispering?' whispered the dwarf. 'Why are we whispering?' he asked again, more loudly.

Cy raised his hand. 'Shhh,' he said. 'Listen.'

There was silence. The dwarf opened his mouth. Cy pressed his fingers to his lips and frowned. 'Wait,' he mouthed silently.

There was nothing. Only the deathly stillness of the great tomb and beyond that the vast emptiness of the desert.

And then they both heard a small sigh.

'I'm out of here,' said the dwarf. 'This is definitely *not* in the programme.'

Cy grabbed the dwarf's arm as he made to leave. 'Wait,' he said. 'He's only a boy.'

'Yes, but he should not be here.' The dwarf prised Cy's fingers from his arm. He turned and looked at Cy for a long moment. 'You have a powerful imagination.'

'But . . . I didn't actually imagine him.'

'You *must* have.'

Cy shook his head. 'I wanted to meet him again, but I didn't dream him up. Did you?'

'No, I did not!' The dwarf stamped his foot. 'I wouldn't be so irresponsible.' He glared at Cy. 'There are *squillions* of dreams passing through time and space and I have the benighted bad luck to end up in one where the Dream Master is under-age and undereducated, and ... and ... under the impression that things can happen in a dream without the dream's Dream Master dreaming it up!'

'Yeah,' agreed Cy. 'Things *have* gone a bit strange.'

'That is an understatement!' said the dwarf and he began to bite his beard.

Cy leant forward and spoke to the figure in the mummy case. 'Can you hear me?' The boy's eyes flickered open. They were blank with terror.

Cy swallowed his own fear and managed to smile. 'Hello,' he said.

The boy opened and closed his mouth several times. 'Who are you?' he managed to say at last.

'Cy,' said Cy.

'Cy.' The boy repeated the word slowly, hesi-tantly. 'What is ... Cy?'

'It's my name,' said Cy. 'It's short for Cyrus.'

The boy made a small whimpering sound. 'Osiris ... God of Death.'

'Oh, no,' said Cy. 'No, I'm not a god.'

The boy nodded fearfully. 'You are here with me in the tomb. Osiris comes at death to judge all people. This I know, as I have been taught by my uncle.'

Cy shook his head and tried to think of a way to explain how he came to be in the tomb. But then he realized that he didn't fully understand it himself. The boy was shaking, whether from fear or cold Cy did not know.

He took the boy gently by the arm. 'Let's talk,' he said. He made a space among the furniture and sat the boy down. Then he held the torch high. 'Look at me,' he said. 'I am a boy just like you. What is your name?'

'I am Aten of the Ankh.' The boy studied Cy carefully, looking at his white T-shirt and red boxer shorts, and his hair, which fell on each side with a middle parting.

'You are a boy,' he said at last, 'but you are not as I am. You are of another people.'

'Yes,' said Cy eagerly. 'I am from another land.'

'Across the great desert?' asked Aten.

'Across the desert,' said Cy, 'and beyond the sea.'

'Then how came you here?' Aten spread his hand out in front of him. 'You must be a god. Only a god can walk through stone.'

'Good point,' said the dwarf in a low voice. 'Answer that, Mr Smartypants.'

Cy ignored him. 'Why are you inside the tomb?' he asked Aten.

Aten frowned. 'For many years there has been great unrest in the land. When the Pharaoh died the court officials decided that his heir was too young to rule, so they decided to crown a new king of their own. My uncle opposed them and I was taken captive with him. We were to be executed, but a great sandstorm arose . . .' He tailed off, and stared at Cy. 'You were there!' he exclaimed. 'I remember now. You came riding from within the bright sun to rescue me.' He looked at the torch in Cy's hand and began to tremble again. 'You carry the sun in your hand. You truly are a god.'

'No,' said Cy firmly. 'I am not. Look, I'll try to explain about it later. Just tell me how you came to be inside the mummy case.'

'They gave me a sleeping potion to drink and left me to await death. Then they carried me here with all the other goods so that I would disappear and no-one would know where. I did not know that they would put me in the Pharaoh's burial place.' He looked around slowly. 'I suppose it is a great honour.'

From beside Cy the dwarf snorted.

'We must get you out of here,' said Cy.

'Can't you think of a more original line than that?' muttered the dwarf.

Aten looked puzzled. 'The priests and the slaves seal the entrance. There is no way out.'

'I can make a doorway,' said Cy. He stared at the nearest wall and concentrated hard. Slowly, very slowly, a door appeared. 'See?' He stood up, torch in hand, and started to walk towards it. He had only taken a few paces when it disappeared again.

'Hey!' Cy turned to the dwarf. 'What gives?'

The dwarf held up the edge of his cloak. The rippling black silk was edged with grey. 'The dream's fading,' he said. 'It's time to go.'

'No,' said Cy. He stared at the wall and determinedly thought of a door. This time the image barely lasted a few seconds before it shimmered away. He turned to the dwarf in alarm. 'We need a door to get out of here.'

'Dreams don't last for ever, Cy,' said the dwarf.

'This one has to go on a bit longer,' said Cy. 'I *must* help Aten.'

The Dream Master's cloak spun out behind him. It was pearly translucent.

'We have to go back now.' The dwarf spoke urgently.

'I can't leave Aten,' said Cy.

The cloak was changing as they spoke. The material was almost transparent.

'Make your choice, then,' said the Dream Master. 'Go now, while you can. Or stay here with him, walled up in this tomb for three thousand years.'

Chapter 8

Cy turned to Aten. 'I'll come back,' he said. Fear grew in Aten's brown eyes. 'Do not leave me.'

The dwarf tugged at Cy's sleeve. 'Look at your torch,' he said. 'You're losing your energy.' Cy looked down. He could barely feel the torch in his hand, and its light was growing dim. 'Leave now, Cy! This very instant! Immediately! At once!'

Cy shook his head trying to clear his thoughts. The Dream Master's voice was getting fainter. 'My dream cloak is fading, I must leave. If you do not

come with me now, then I cannot help you.'

Cy felt his strength ebbing away. There was a place where the dream had thinned out and he could see his bedroom. He tried to focus his eyes. Yes ... there was the chest of drawers, the bed, walls and carpet. They were all moving slowly, with a gentle swaying motion. And then Cy realized what was happening. His dream was drifting away, and if he stayed he would be carried off inside it. He had to return to his own room in the next few seconds, or he would never get another chance. And now in front of him there was a tear, a ragged hole in the fabric, which he could pass through. Cy stretched out his fingers.

'Do not depart, O great God Osiris,' begged Aten.

'I am not a god,' Cy said wretchedly. He moved towards the space in his dream and then stopped. He turned to the dwarf and shook his head. 'I can't go.'

'Oh, yes you *can*.' The dwarf stepped forwards to give Cy an almighty push in the back.

As he did so, Aten suddenly noticed the amulet looped around Cy's wrist.

'My ankh!' he cried. 'You must not take away my spirit! Give me back my amulet!' And, at the very instant Cy fell through the gap in his dream back into his own bedroom, Aten lunged forward and grabbed hold of his wrist. The two of them landed in a desperate tangle of bedclothes, and tumbled onto the floor.

'Cy!'

'Shhh!' Cy told Aten as they struggled to their feet.

'I did not speak,' replied Aten. He looked around him in disbelief. 'This is your home?'

'Cy!' came the shout once again, more urgently, and Cy recognized his mother's voice. She was right outside his room!

Cy glanced around wildly. 'The cupboard!' And opening the door of his bedroom cupboard he bundled Aten inside.

'Cy, we've all overslept,' his mother said as she came into his room.

'Uh-huh,' said Cy, his head still inside the cupboard. 'I was just getting my gear together.' He grabbed a hanger, and slamming his cupboard door shut, he turned with his back against it and a manic grin on his face. 'I'll be right there.'

'Good boy. It's all your dad's fault. He said he had an odd dream. That he was a Pharaoh in Ancient Egypt . . .' His mum peered at the hanger.

'Haven't you got a clean school shirt?'

Cy looked down at the hanger and the Frankenstein T-shirt draped across it. 'Yes.' He flung the hanger on the bed and snatched a shirt from among some clean laundry which his mother had placed in his room days ago. 'Got it right here. Absolutely, no probs,' he babbled.

'Right, fast as you can. I'll make you a sandwich to eat as you walk to school.'

Aten stepped slowly out of the cupboard, and gazed in bewilderment at Cy's bedroom. His look took in the piles of clothes, books, magazines, CDs, tapes, spaceships, models, boots, games, rucksack and, in the corner, a sportsbag spewing football kit.

'The priests have lied to us,' said Aten. 'This is not the Afterlife as they said it would be. The land of the gods should be peaceful, with green oases, running water and fountains.'

'Well,' said Cy, rushing around trying to find his trousers and tie. 'This isn't the afterlife, exactly. It's more the . . . the . . . *forward-life*.'

Aten stepped carefully over a stack of comics. 'Why do all your garments lie upon the ground?'

'You sound like my mother,' said Cy, pulling on his trainers.

'Why do you have so many clothes?' asked

Aten. 'Why are they so heavy? Are your winters very cold?'

'And the summers,' said Cy. 'Look, don't ask me so many questions. It's nearly time for school and I haven't a clue what I'm going to do with you. You'll have to stay in my room today. Hide in the cupboard until Mum and Dad leave for work and then you can come out.' He looked at Aten's short linen kilt, and started pulling open drawers. 'I'll need to find you something to wear in case anybody sees you.' He held up trainers, a sweatshirt and jogging bottoms. 'What about these?'

'The shoes are a good size,' said Aten. 'But the clothes will not fit very well. I am a bit taller than you.'

'CY! HURRY UP, WILL YOU!'

Cy leapt in panic as Lauren's voice screeched right outside his room door.

'Don't come in!' Cy shouted, but he was too late.

His bedroom door crashed open, and his sister Lauren stood there. 'Mum says—' She broke off in mid-sentence, then she pointed a bright blue fingernail at Aten. 'Where,' she demanded, 'did *he* come from?'

Chapter 9

'Get out of my room!' Cy yelled.

Lauren held up her hands. 'Take it easy, Cyberman. I was sent to hurry you up.'

'Well, you knock first in future,' shouted Cy. 'Aten was ... was ... trying out his Egyptian costume for the school show.'

'I didn't hear him come into the house,' said Lauren, backing out of the door.

'I let him in the front door,' said Cy. 'Not that it's any of *your* business. Tell Mum we'll be down in a minute,' he shouted after her.

When his sister had closed the bedroom door behind her, Cy turned to Aten. 'I thought that you could stay in my room for the day. But now that Lauren's seen you, you'll have to come to school with me.'

'School?' said Aten. 'I did not hope for school in the land of the gods.'

'For the nineteenth time! This is *not* the land of the gods!' Cy sat down on the edge of his bed. How could he prepare an Ancient Egyptian for modern life in ... he glanced at his watch ... in about sixty seconds? 'Do you know anything about science?' Cy asked Aten. 'About how things work?'

'I know a little. Scientists are very clever, so I do not understand all of it.'

'Neither do I,' said Cy. 'But there are lots of things around because of science, or scientific inventions. Like ... like ...' Cy tried to think of something that the Ancient Egyptians used. 'For instance saws, to saw wood. Right?'

Aten nodded slowly.

'So, as we're a bit further on than you, we've invented more things. OK? Everything you'll see and hear today is just science. It is very advanced science. And ... and I'll try to explain later how it all works.' Cy looked at the books on the shelf above his desk, and grabbed one on transport. 'When we go outside,' he went on, 'it will be *very* loud. There are chariots without horses, hundreds of them. They have lots of different shapes, some are huge. And they make a lot of noise. Look.'

Aten's eyes opened wide as he looked at the illustrations and the text in the book. He fingered the pages, he touched the surface and rubbed at the print. 'What ink is this?'

'Special ink,' said Cy.

Aten spread his fingers and traced the shapes of the letters. 'What does it say?'

Cy leant over and read, 'Modern roads are now clogged with so much traffic that, during the rush hour in major cities, people progress more slowly than if they were using horse-drawn vehicles in the Middle Ages.' He stopped reading and frowned. 'I didn't realize that,' he said.

Aten looked at the page and then back to Cy. 'You can read these symbols so quickly?'

'My reading is not too bad,' said Cy. 'It's my writing that's the problem.'

'Me too,' said Aten. 'Malik, the chief scribe, told me I was the worst pupil he had ever taught.'

Cy grinned. Where had he heard that before?

'Come on,' he said. 'Put on those clothes and let's get out of here.'

'Mum,' said Cy, as he opened the kitchen door, 'Aten's here. He came round for me this morning.'

'Oh, right. Hello . . . er . . . Aten,' said Cy's mum as she handed Cy his sandwich. Then she caught sight of Lauren as she slid past her towards the back door. 'Do you have to wear so much eye-shadow to school, Lauren? I'm sure it's not allowed.'

Cy's dad dragged a wad of paper hankies from a box on the worktop and pressed them into Lauren's hand. 'Remove aforesaid make-up before exiting building,' he instructed her.

'You two are totally *boring*,' Lauren complained loudly, as she dabbed at her eyelids. She flung the tissues in the bin and flounced out. 'BORING!'

'Try to catch her up, boys.' Cy's dad winked at them. 'But don't get too close.'

When they reached the main road Lauren ducked into the first bus shelter, took out her make-up mirror and began re-applying her purple eye-shadow.

Aten stopped and stared at her. 'Your sister is like a wondrous goddess,' Aten said to Cy.

Lauren turned around. 'What did you say?' she demanded suspiciously.

'That you are most beautiful,' Aten repeated sincerely. 'Queen Nefertiti herself did not have colours of such brilliance.'

'What?'

Aten nodded solemnly. 'The plumage of the birds in the bulrushes by the great river fade beside your glory.'

'Eh?' said Lauren, whose face was now pink.

'Cool it,' said Cy from the side of his mouth.

Aten stared up at the cloudy sky. 'I am not warm,' he said.

'It is nothing to do with being warm. It means . . .' Cy stopped. What *did* 'cool' actually mean? 'I'd better teach you a few things to say when people speak to you,' he told Cy. 'First of all, if anyone says "What's the story?" you say, "Morning glory", and, if you want to be really friendly, you slap them hard on the back.'

Aten looked again at the sky. 'Your morning is not glorious.'

'Never mind that,' said Cy. 'It doesn't have anything to do with the time of day.'

'Cool is not the opposite of warm, and morning does not mean morning.' Aten spoke slowly.

'Your language is very strange.'

'Our language is . . .' Cy stopped as a thought occurred to him. Language . . . 'How is it that you can speak my language, Aten?'

'I am not speaking your language. You are speaking mine.'

'No,' said Cy. 'I can't.'

'But I understand what you say to me,' said Aten. 'At least, I recognize some of the words. Most of what you tell me does not make sense. I am very confused. However, it is more pleasant to be here than in the tomb.' He smiled happily.

Cy shook his head. He didn't like to tell Aten that most of what was happening to *him* at the moment didn't make sense.

'Just go with me on this,' said Cy. 'They are ways of saying things. But they don't exactly mean what they say, it's a . . . a . . . figure of speech, or like . . . slang. You must have used slang when you spoke to your friends.'

'Ah!' said Aten. 'I know what you mean. In our town one of the favourite expressions of the young scribes was: "And the water buffaloes will dance with the crocodiles in the corn under a harvest moon." '

There was a silence.

'And what does that mean, exactly?' enquired Cy after a few moments.

'Well, it indicates that the person has lied or is exaggerating.' Aten looked at Cy. 'I didn't think about it before, but language is very peculiar. There is another popular saying which is used in many ways: "The length of a man's life in the desert is measured by the amount of water in his camel."'

'Really?' said Cy politely. 'Em . . . ours is shorter. We have one word to cover every situation. If in doubt say "cool".'

'Shool,' repeated Aten.

'No,' said Cy. 'Like this. Cool. Say it as if it begins with a K.'

'Chay?' said Aten.

'Try again,' said Cy. 'C-O-O-L.' He spelt it out. 'But it's got a hard C so you pronounce it as if it begins with a K.'

Aten gave him a puzzled look. 'You say it begins with a C but I have to pretend that it begins with a K? If you pronounce it as a K then why not spell it with a K? Why should it be different? Your language is strange. In our picture writing it is the same symbol – a basket.'

'Well, your writing is much more sensible than

ours,' said Cy. 'Ours is really stupid. You'll never believe how they spell *"thorough"*. The whole writing–spelling thing is an absolute mess. The best thing is not to think about it too much, just do it.' He gave Aten an encouraging smile. 'Try again. Cool.'

'Call?' Aten tried cautiously.

'Cooooool,' said Cy.

'Coo-el,' Aten repeated.

'Great! Now, nod your head when you're saying it.'

Aten wagged his head up and down frantically.

'No, more relaxed, and kind of side to side,' said Cy. 'And try to look casual when you're doing it.' Cy stuck his hands in his pockets, hunched his shoulders and lolled against the bus shelter. 'Like this.'

Aten copied Cy carefully. He slouched against the bus shelter, and shook his head slowly from side to side while moving it up and down.

'Cool.' He rolled the word out proudly. 'Cooooooool. Coo-*elll*.'

'*Brilliant*,' said Cy.

Lauren lowered her make-up mirror and stared at them both. 'What on *earth* are you two doing?'

Cy and Aten straightened up at once. 'Nothing,' they said together.

'Come *on*, then,' Lauren said impatiently. 'I can't wait any longer for you.'

Aten raised his eyebrows and Cy shrugged.

'We have another phrase,' said Aten as the boys hurried after Cy's sister. ' "By the walls of the temple the cats are wailing." '

'Which means?'

Aten gave Cy an innocent smile. 'It means that the cats are wailing by the walls of the temple,' he replied.

Cy stared at Aten. 'Eh?'

Aten started to laugh. 'I make a joke,' he said. 'Egyptian humour. Ha! Ha!'

'Oh, right,' said Cy.

Aten laughed even louder. He pointed at Cy. 'Your face,' he said. 'The expression is so funny.'

Ahead of him Cy could see the road junction and the crossing patrol. Now he had to think of a way to get Aten into school for the day. He glanced at Aten, who was still guffawing with laughter. Cy tried to smile, but didn't succeed. One of his dad's favourite expressions had just popped into his head: 'This is no laughing matter.'

Chapter 10

It was in fact Mrs Chalmers, Cy's teacher, who came to the rescue. She was usually in class before the bell rang and Cy went straight there with Aten.

'Mrs Chalmers,' Cy took a deep breath. 'Would it be OK if Aten stayed in your class in school today? He's visiting. My mum wrote a note. I've got it here somewhere.' Cy started to search in his pockets . . . very slowly.

'I didn't realize the foreign exchange pupils

had started to arrive already.' Mrs Chalmers smiled at Aten.

'Foreign exchange pupils,' Cy repeated. 'Of course! Aten is a . . . yes . . . a bit early arriving here. There . . . there was a mix up with his travel arrangements.' Cy uncrossed his fingers behind his back. That last bit was true anyway. 'My mum was hoping he could spend some time in school with me while she sorted things out for him.' He began to empty his rucksack onto his desk. Orange peel, pencil case, carton of juice, crisps, books, jotter. Hopelessly, Cy prodded among them.

'It should be all right,' said Mrs Chalmers. 'I'll take the letter along to the office and check with the Head.' She came to help Cy look for the letter, picking up his books and fanning out the pages. 'Did you see Cy's letter from his mum?' she asked Aten.

'I cannot say that I did,' Aten replied carefully.

The first bell for assembly rang. Mrs Chalmers glanced at her watch. 'We'll find it later. Cy, you run along quickly and I'll take Aten to sign in and get a visitor's badge.'

'I'll come and help,' said Cy. 'Aten's English isn't good, and . . . and he's never been in a foreign country before.'

'That's not quite true,' Aten interrupted. 'I journeyed by camel caravan to Nubia some years ago.'

'Eh?' Cy frowned at Aten.

'That's absolutely fascinating!' exclaimed Mrs Chalmers. 'You will be able to tell the class all about it later.' She put her hand on Cy's shoulder and steered him firmly towards the door. 'We'll catch up with you later, Cy.'

Camel caravans in Nubia! Omigollygosh! Cy looked back anxiously. What else would Aten say? If he started telling them that Cy had rescued him from a tomb in Ancient Egypt then they would probably lock him up. Or lock Cy up. Or lock both of them. *And* throw away the key.

'Don't panic, don't panic, don't panic,' Cy chanted in a low voice as he ran along to the assembly hall.

Miss Fullbright, the head teacher, had already begun the morning prayer. Cy slipped in at the back and found a seat about halfway down on the right hand side, at the end of a row next to the wall.

As Cy listened to the Head's voice droning on in assembly he kept glancing towards the double doors at the back. After about five minutes Mrs

Chalmers slipped in at the back. Aten wasn't with her. What had happened to him? Cy craned his neck. No sign of Aten. She was definitely on her own. Where was he? Maybe Aten had just disappeared into the atmosphere. He was really only part of a dream anyway, wasn't he? Cy looked around him. Maybe all of this was a dream. Was he, in fact, imagining this assembly? The Head was now reading out the weekly good conduct list and Vicky, sitting on Cy's left, was swinging her legs restlessly. Was Vicky actually there? And how would he know if it was a dream anyway? You never really knew until you woke up. Cy reached up and touched his eyes. He was definitely awake.

Vicky caught his eye and grinned. 'She *does* go on,' she whispered, nodding at the stage.

Cy nodded back absent-mindedly. Perhaps if he concentrated really hard he could imagine himself back in the Pharaoh's tomb. He looked at the Egyptian wall frieze on the right hand wall just beside him. The river Nile with the outline of a funeral barge, two priests in attendance. The great Sphinx at Giza, with the desert stretching endlessly away. The Pharaoh in his chariot, the plumed horses. The border along the bottom made up of Egyptian symbols, a scarab beetle, a sceptre, the boy with the ankh . . .

The ankh!

Cy's mouth fell open. The ankh was no longer round the boy's neck. Very slowly Cy lifted up his own hand. Still wrapped round his wrist was Aten's ankh. Cy touched it carefully with his other hand. Mrs Chalmers had told him that it was a magical symbol for the Ancient Egyptians. Cy remembered Aten's terror when he realized that it no longer hung round his neck. What had he called it? 'My soul . . . my spirit'? What special powers could it have? Cy fingered it gently.

'Don't touch that!' hissed a voice on his right.

Cy turned and looked at the Egyptian wall frieze. From underneath his head-dress one of the priests glared at him ferociously.

'Dream Master!' yelped Cy.

The dwarf put his fingers to his lips. 'Shhh!'

'What are you doing here?' Cy whispered out of the side of his mouth.

'Trying to fix your filthy foul-up!' snarled the dwarf. 'Meantime, do not touch that ankh. You will only make matters worse.'

'How?' asked Cy. His fingers brushed against the little amulet.

'It has come through from the Dreamworld so it

will have special power in this TimeSpace,' said the dwarf. 'But nothing like this has ever happened before so I don't know what exactly.'

'What are you going to do?'

'The matter requires some thought.'

'You mean, you don't know what to do?' asked Cy.

'I am developing a strategy,' said the dwarf.

'Omigosh,' said Cy. 'You *really* don't know.'

'There is *nothing* a Dream Master doesn't know!' the dwarf snapped back. 'How dare—'

'Cyrus Peters . . .'

'What?' Cyrus jumped as Vicky elbowed him sharply.

The head teacher had just said his name.

Cy sat up and stared at the stage with a fixed smile.

'. . . friend from abroad,' continued Miss Fullbright. 'And while other arrangements are being made he will spend some time with us. Now I would like you all to welcome Aten.'

Everyone began to clap. Cy gripped the edge of his seat. This couldn't be happening! Aten was on the stage, in front of the whole school!

'Mrs Chalmers has told me that Aten has had some interesting experiences.' Miss Fullbright smiled kindly at Aten. Aten smiled back.

Cy's own smile became a grimace.

'In particular,' Miss Fullbright went on, 'I believe that you went on an expedition with a camel caravan across the desert?'

'Indeed, yes,' Aten nodded confidently. 'My uncles own many, many camels. They trade perfumes and ebony wood, gold and incense.'

'Perhaps you would like to tell us a little about it?' suggested Miss Fullbright.

'I would be honoured,' said Aten.

In the audience, Cy whimpered.

'Well then, young man,' said the Head. She stood back to usher Aten to the front of the stage. 'What's your story?'

Aten gave a huge grin. He stepped forward. 'Morning glory!' he said in a loud voice, and, reaching out, he gave Miss Fullbright a resounding thump on the back.

Chapter 11

Cy had never known his head teacher to lose her composure. Not ever. Even on the day he had seen her separate two dogs fighting in the playground she had managed to look calm, efficient, and in charge. She didn't now.

Partly it was because her half-moon reading glasses shot right off and landed on the head of one of the infants sitting in the front row. Otherwise, Cy thought, she might have recovered more quickly. But, by the time the small, quaking child had handed them back up to her, Aten had

got to the bit about the camels breaking wind. Cy slid down in his seat as the hall erupted in laughter.

Aten looked puzzled. He had been trying to explain how sensible it was not to be at the end of the camel train when this happened. He called it 'blowing air' but, as he had also used sound effects, no-one was in any doubt what he meant. It was soon after that, and just when he had got started on how much his uncle had paid for the slaves he had brought from beyond the Red Land, that Miss Fullbright interrupted to thank Aten very firmly, and say, although all of this was absolutely fascinating, they didn't have an awful lot of time left, and no doubt Mrs Chalmers had some things which she wanted to show Aten right now. She then signalled urgently for Mrs Chalmers to come and take Aten away. Cy could see his teacher's shoulders shaking as she walked up the aisle. The Head didn't look too pleased, but everybody else thought it was brilliant.

Later, when Cy got to his classroom after assembly, Mrs Chalmers had already given Aten some books to look at while she did the morning class work. Cy heard her explaining to Aten that it was not the normal British custom to slap a schoolteacher on the back and shout 'Morning glory!' at the top of your voice. Especially not the head teacher, and definitely not in morning assembly.

Nevertheless, Cy had to admit that Aten's story had been extremely interesting. And, as Vicky pointed out, it *had* livened up a very boring assembly.

However, it had also done exactly what Cy hadn't wanted to do. Made everyone notice Aten. Instead of keeping Aten quietly in class for a day until he could ask Grampa what to do, Aten was now the centre of attention. It didn't help that he was also fascinated by his trouser pockets and kept insisting on pulling them to the *outside* of the legs.

During break-time everyone they met laughed and called out, 'Morning glory.' Even the infant kids whispered and pointed.

Unfortunately it also attracted the type of attention that Cy normally went out of his way to avoid. Just as break was finishing they ran into the Mean Machines in the corridor.

'Well, hello, camel boy,' Chloe said nastily.

'Well. Hello. Yourself,' Aten replied cautiously.

'Considering all these famous uncles of yours traded in gold, you don't seem to have very good clothes to wear,' sneered Eddie. 'They don't even fit you properly.' He pointed to Aten's wrists sticking out the sleeves of the sweatshirt which Aten was wearing.

'Lay off,' said Cy, in what he hoped was a commanding tone of voice.

Eddie turned to Cy with wide eyes. 'Oh . . . and who's going to make me?' he demanded.

'You lot behaving yourselves?' Mrs Chalmers had come up behind them on her way from the staff room.

'We were just talking to Aten, Mrs Chalmers,' said Chloe quickly.

'That's nice,' said Mrs Chalmers. 'The Head will be pleased that Aten is being taken good care of.'

'Oh, we'll look after him properly.' Eddie gave his teacher his most innocent smile.

'And the water buffaloes will dance with the crocodiles in the corn under a harvest moon,' Aten murmured.

'Water buffaloes with crocodiles, Aten?' said Mrs Chalmers as she walked with them back to the classroom. 'That's not very likely, is it?'

Aten gave Cy's teacher a long look. 'Exactly,' he said.

'Ah,' said Mrs Chalmers thoughtfully, and her

eyes followed Eddie and Chloe as they went back to their seats.

At lunch-time Cy led Aten away from the crowded playground. Avoiding the path that led to the river, which was strictly out of bounds, they walked towards the sports fields.

'After school I'm going to ask Grampa what to do,' said Cy, sitting down on the grass and opening his lunch-bag.

'Yes,' Aten nodded. 'The very old are very wise.'

Cy thought for a minute. Although Cy knew that Grampa had fought in the last war it had never struck him before about Grampa being old. 'I'll ask him if he'll let you stay with him while I figure out how to get you back into my dream,' he told Aten.

'I day-dream a lot,' said Aten. 'Malik, the chief scribe shouts at me all the time to pay attention. I find it hard to concentrate when I am being taught.'

'Me too,' said Cy. He offered Aten a peanut-butter sandwich.

Aten took it and, peeling back the top slice, he inspected the filling carefully. 'What is this, exactly?' he enquired.

'Peanut butter,' said Cy. He bit into his own. 'Go on,' he urged, 'you'll like it.'

'One is reminded of following the camel caravan,' said Aten. He nibbled the edge of his bread very delicately.

They were almost at the boundary fence where the playing-fields of the secondary school ran alongside the primary school.

'Oh, look,' said Aten. 'Your sister Lauren, with some of her friends. How pleasant.'

Cy looked to where Aten pointed, ' "Pleasant" and "Lauren" don't belong in the same sentence,' said Cy. He picked up his rucksack and got to his feet. 'Let's go. Fast.'

'Hey, small person,' called Lauren. 'Stop right there. I want to talk to you.'

'No,' said Cy over his shoulder. 'I don't want to talk to you.'

'You'd better wait,' his sister yelled louder. 'There's rumours going about that Aten broke up your morning assembly.'

'So what?'

'They're also saying that he's one of Mum's foreign exchange pupils. Did you tell them that, little brother?'

'It's none of your business,' said Cy.

'Oh, yes, it is,' said Lauren. 'We've found out about him, anyway.'

'Yeah.' Baz nodded. 'We know.'

'Absolutely,' agreed Cartwheel.

'What?' Cy asked nervously. 'You know what, exactly?'

'That Mum didn't recognize him this morning,' said Lauren. 'So that means that Aten shouldn't be here, not officially, anyway. You've been telling lies.' Cy's heart gave a terrific lurch and he gazed at his sister. 'You'd better come clean, Cyberman, and tell us. Who is Aten, and where does he come from?'

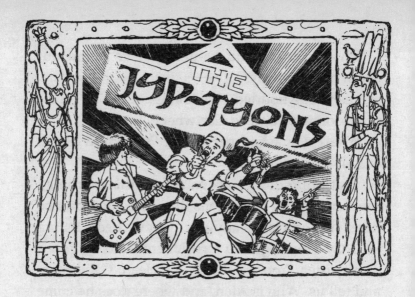

Chapter 12

'It's a secret,' said Cy.

Lauren grabbed Cy by the neck. 'Brothers and sisters shouldn't have secrets from each other.'

'Oh yeah?' said Cy, struggling to free himself. 'You never tell *me* anything. So, since when did that rule apply?'

'Since I decided it just this minute,' said Lauren, giving Cy another shake.

'To save disagreement,' said Aten, 'perhaps I should tell your sister and her friends exactly

who I am and where I came from.'

'No!' cried Cy. He twisted free from Lauren's grip. 'No way,' he said. 'This lot would tell everybody, and it would cause *so* much trouble.'

'I think perhaps, at this moment, *not* to tell them will cause more trouble,' said Aten. 'Let me explain . . .' He stretched out one hand, palm facing outwards. 'I offer truth as a gift, yours for the taking.'

'Oh, no,' said Cy. He sat down on the grass with his head in his hands.

'Your brother rescued me from some rather nasty people who would have done me harm,' said Aten.

'Nasty people?' repeated Lauren. 'What kind of people? What kind of harm? Who are you?'

'I am an Egyptian. We are quite famous. Perhaps you have heard of us?'

The girls stared at Aten for a second or two.

'Of course we've heard of the Egyptians,' said Cartwheel, 'but that doesn't explai—'

She was interrupted by a sudden shriek from Baz. 'The Egyptians!' Baz dug her nails into Lauren's arm. 'I know who he is! He's one of the *Jyp-Tyons*. I think it's a new Boy Band from Egypt. Their music's more funky rock with a bit of sixties retro. The lead singer's got his head shaved with a pony-tail growing out of the side. Cool!'

'Cool,' agreed Aten. He nodded his head and shrugged his shoulders.

Lauren turned to her brother. 'Why didn't you say?' she demanded.

'Because ... because ... they don't want any publicity. They'd get mobbed by weenies.'

'Why is he with you in school?'

'He asked me to take him. He wanted to see what our schools were like. Primary schools,' Cy added quickly. '*Not* secondary schools.'

'Where did you meet him?'

'At the youth club. In the community centre.' Cy's brain was exhausted trying to keep ahead in this game where he had to invent something new with each sentence. 'Enough,' he said quickly. 'I'm not answering any more questions.'

At once the girls surrounded Aten.

'What are you doing here?' asked Baz.

Aten lifted his hand and showed them his sandwich. 'I am eating a strange substance which, much to my surprise, is not camel droppings.'

'Why are you here? Where are you staying?' demanded Cartwheel.

Aten glanced at Cy. 'I think I will stay with

grandfather,' he said slowly. 'And I am here because . . . because I am not somewhere else.'

The girls giggled.

'The things you say. They're really funny,' said Cartwheel.

Aten looked puzzled. 'I speak only the truth.'

'You mustn't blab about this,' Cy pleaded. 'It wouldn't be good for Aten if everybody knew about him. And anyway, he's going away soon.'

Lauren looked at Cy with narrowed eyes. 'You can't fool us,' she said. 'His band are obviously here for a gig. We want free tickets.'

Cy thought quickly. 'OK,' he said. 'You'll get the first tickets available, I promise. But only on the condition that you say nothing to anyone, and you back me up with Mrs Chalmers so that he can stay in school for a couple of days.'

'You're on,' said Lauren.

'You must tell no-one,' said Cy.

'You know you can trust us,' said Lauren.

'Absolutely,' said Cartwheel.

'For ever,' said Baz.

'Our lips are sealed,' said Lauren.

'Omigosh,' moaned Cy, as the girls went off towards their playing-fields. Nightmare city or what? He turned to Aten. 'It will be all over the school in an hour,' he said. 'Why did you let them believe that junk about a group called the *Jyp-Tyons*?'

'At no time did I lie,' said Aten.

'You did so!' said Cy. 'When they babbled on about you being part of a boy band, you agreed with them.'

'I did not. The only thing I said was the word "cool", which, according to you, can mean anything. In this case I intended it to mean, "not at all, what you say is completely wrong."' Despite himself, Cy laughed out loud. Aten raised his eyebrows. 'As I said, truth is a gift offered. Although,' Aten paused, 'it is sometimes not offered alone. One has to choose carefully. There can be dung amongst dates. Your sister and her friends selected the truth they wished to hear.'

As Aten and Cy walked back towards the playground, Aten turned to Cy. 'What is this Boy Band?' he asked. 'And what is a gig, exactly?'

Chapter 13

'**W**e're going to the assembly hall for a rehearsal for our Egyptian play this afternoon,' said Mrs Chalmers after lunch-break. 'I've put most of the scenery in the cupboard along there now. Aten, you might be able to give us some helpful advice with the costumes and props.'

'Just be careful what you say,' said Cy to Aten as the class went along the corridor. 'It's better that nobody finds out where you came from. Don't tell any more wild stories

about caravans and sandstorms.'

'I will guard my tongue,' said Aten.

In the hall Cy looked again at the wall frieze. The boy scribe looked more calm now, as he sat in the sand with his reed pen and brushes.

Aten pointed to the broken pottery pieces and stones which lay in the sand beside him. 'These are called *ostraca*,' he said. 'It is what we practise on, until the chief scribe decides that we are ready to write upon papyrus.'

'A bit like us using scrap paper,' said Mrs Chalmers. 'But you should have said "practised" not "practise" in that sentence, Aten, because you are talking about something that happened in the past.'

'No, truly,' began Aten, 'we write every day—'

'Day . . .' Cy spoke fast. 'Day . . . te. Date, that is. Aten writes down every date in a diary . . . which he keeps . . . a sort of travel diary. It's a project he's doing, like a report he has to write.'

'Do I?' said Aten.

'Yes,' said Cy. He dragged Aten by the arm. 'Let's go and help Basra and Vicky get the costume rail and scenery from the stage cupboard.'

'Tell them to be quick,' Mrs Chalmers called after them. 'No day-dreaming!'

'Our teachers say the same words,' said Aten as they crossed the hall. 'But when my teacher is angry with me I tell him one of my jokes and that makes him smile.'

'Does it really?' said Cy. He began to help Basra drag out the huge cardboard pyramid which was their main prop for the play.

'Yes,' said Aten. 'My friends all laugh when I tell my stories.'

Basra peered round from behind the papier mâché mummy. He crossed his eyes at Cy. 'I'm not surprised,' he said.

'I know a joke,' said Vicky. 'What do you call a dinosaur with sunglasses?'

Aten narrowed his eyes. 'Dino-saur . . . with . . . sunglasses . . . ? I do not know. What is the answer?'

'D'you-think-he-sawrus?'

'Ah,' said Aten. He glanced at Cy. 'Em . . . Cool?' He nodded slowly once or twice. 'I too have a riddle,' he said. 'If your dog Sut has no tail, what do you call him?'

'Don't know,' said Vicky.

'Sut,' said Aten.

'Oh, ha-ha,' said Vicky.

'Egyptian humour is very funny,' said Aten. 'My

uncle, who deals in ostrich feathers, knows many tales told by the traders in the slave markets of Nubia.'

'Aten, you are very similar to Cy,' said Mrs Chalmers, who had come over to hurry them up. 'You have a powerful imagination.' She smiled. 'But you have to be careful, and not tell whoppers about trading slaves.'

Aten opened his mouth, and then closed it quickly as he saw Cy frowning at him.

'You can sit and watch us perform,' said Mrs Chalmers, 'or perhaps you might help with the music. Could you manage to play a simple instrument?'

'I don't think that's a good idea,' said Cy at once.

'Wouldn't you like to join in?' Mrs Chalmers asked Aten.

'I would like that very much,' said Aten.

'You wouldn't enjoy it,' said Cy.

'Yes, I would,' said Aten.

'No,' said Cy.

'Oh good. That's settled then,' said Mrs Chalmers. She handed Aten the triangle and stick. 'Just give that a little rap now and then, when you think it appropriate.' She clapped her hands. 'Let's start the Procession of the Pharaoh.'

Cy was glad that he had a very minor part in the show, as it meant he could keep an eye on Aten standing at the side with the musicians. He had seen Chloe and Eddie glancing in their direction and talking together earlier. Cy knew that when the Mean Machines started whispering they were usually picking victims, and it was better to keep a low profile. Aten wasn't helping with this at all. He was always doing something different. During rehearsal, when Mrs Chalmers pointed at him for his musical cue, instead of giving a quick *ting* on the triangle, he performed a little musical tune.

'Oh, very good, Aten!' cried Mrs Chalmers. Aten gave a little bow.

'Oh, terrific!' said Cy under his breath as he saw Chloe make a face at Eddie.

At the end of the rehearsal Mrs Chalmers was very pleased. 'Well done, everybody!' she said. 'Next Friday afternoon is going to be spectacular. There are only one or two minor things to sort out. And, of course, we still have to make the mask of King Tutankhamun. You know,' Mrs Chalmers looked at Aten carefully, 'your face would be an excellent model for it, Aten.'

'I have not heard of this king, Tut-Ankh-Amun,' said Aten.

'He is one of the most very famous,' said Vicky. 'Although very young he was very wise. He was much more tolerant than previous rulers.'

'He was not so young as we imagine,' said Mrs Chalmers. 'People matured much more quickly then. It was not uncommon to be married at twelve years old.'

'No way!' said Vicky.

'Can you come to school tomorrow?' Mrs Chalmers asked Aten. 'And if you don't mind, we could plaster cast your face for our golden mask.'

'It would be an honour,' said Aten.

Mrs Chalmers organized the clearing up. 'Musicians, take your instruments to the music base, everyone else carry something along to the classroom. Cy and Aten, would you please put the large props back in the cupboard under the stage?'

Eddie and Chloe exchanged glances. 'We'll help with the mummy and the pyramid,' said Eddie.

Cy regarded him suspiciously. 'There's a first time for everything,' he muttered under his breath. Then he saw Chloe nudge Eddie. 'I'm not going under the stage with you two,' Cy said firmly.

Mrs Chalmers looked across from the other side of the hall. 'Eddie, Chloe,' she called, 'why don't you take these script sheets back to the classroom.

I'm sure Aten and Cy will manage on their own.'

Mrs Chalmers began to manoeuvre the big pyramid towards the stage cupboard as Eddie and Chloe left the hall. Then the school secretary put his head round the door. 'There's a telephone call for you, Mrs Chalmers,' he said.

'Righto.' Mrs Chalmers spoke to Cy. 'The final bell will go in a minute or two,' she said. 'I'm going to go and dismiss the rest of the class quickly. Can you manage the rest of the props?' She hurried out of the hall.

Cy bent low and pushed the costume clothes-rail ahead of him into the stage cupboard. Then he crawled in, dragging the mummy case behind him. 'Can you push the pyramid in,' he shouted over his shoulder at Aten. Aten knelt down, and cautiously pushing the cardboard pyramid ahead of him, he followed Cy under the stage.

Unnoticed by either of them the door of the assembly hall opened a fraction and Chloe and Eddie slipped back in.

Cy shuffled the mummy around to make more room.

'I do not like to be in here,' whispered Aten. 'It reminds me of the tomb of the Pharaoh.'

'Well let's just shove the pyramid into that corner and we'll go.'

Cy reached round to help Aten. As he did so the light from main hall caught the polished silver surface of the ankh tied round his wrist and a wink of light reflected in the gloom.

'Oh . . .' breathed Aten. 'You still wear my ankh. I had forgotten about it.' He reached out to touch it.

Cy blinked. 'Look,' he said hoarsely. The shaft of light touching the ankh seemed suddenly to burn more fiercely, and in doing so it lit up one side of the pyramid. Then, between the long blocks of stone, a door appeared.

Aten clutched his throat. The door had begun to open slowly.

'Come on!' ordered the familiar voice of the Dream Master. 'You have no idea of the amount of bending of non-dimensional space I've had to do in order to try and sort this out. Get yourselves over here.'

Aten stared at Cy, and mouthed the words, 'I do not want to.'

'Er,' said Cy. 'Can we talk about this?'

'There is nothing to talk about.' The dwarf stood at the doorway into the pyramid, and pointed to

Aten. 'You have to return to your own time. That's it. Zero Option. Non-Negotiable. Discussion Discounted.'

Aten shook his head.

'Aten would like to wait on here a bit longer,' said Cy.

The dwarf folded his arms. 'Tell me,' he demanded, 'what part of the word "NO" is it that you don't understand?' He looked very hard at Aten. 'Listen to me, Aten, and understand this. You *must* return to your appointed place. These things are . . . as these things are.' The Dream Master held open his cloak. 'Come.'

Aten broke free of the Dream Master's gaze and he turned to Cy. 'I will take my ankh,' he said.

Cy looked from the Dream Master to Aten. Something had passed between them which he did not exactly understand. He held up the amulet and, without thinking, Cy spun the ankh in his hand. The beam of light wavered and dipped.

'Watch what you're doing with that!' snapped the Dream Master.

'Why?' asked Cy. He held up his wrist and began to untie the ankh. 'I must give it back to Aten.' He shifted his position to lean across to Aten.

'No, don't do that,' said the dwarf urgently. 'Give it to me first, and I will return it to him. I will guard it until it is safely back in its own time.'

Cy stopped. There was real fear in the eyes of the Dream Master. Cy looked again at the ankh. What power did it contain to make the Dream Master himself sound so scared?

'Cy,' said the Dream Master, 'I move through TimeSpace using my dreamcloak. There are other ways, more random, unpredictable. The ankh, which has been taken from its own time, could be used to bend dimensions. But if that happens, then *I will not be there.*' The dwarf held Cy's gaze. 'It would be very dangerous.'

Cy hesitated, and for a moment the silver amulet swung loosely in the air. The next instant he was roughly pushed aside. A hand reached from behind him, grabbed the ankh and snatched it from his grasp. Then the stage cupboard door slammed shut and they heard the catch being dropped into place.

Chapter 14

ten let out the most awful howl.

'Shhh!' yelled Cy.

'We are trapped in the tomb!' cried Aten.

'No, we aren't,' said Cy, trying to sound braver than he felt. 'We are in the cupboard under the stage. Someone has closed the cupboard door on us, and it doesn't take a genius to work out who.'

Aten looked at the pyramid. 'Where is he who summoned us?'

'I'll explain later,' said Cy. 'If I ever work it out myself,' he added under his breath. 'Now,' he

groped his way in the semi-darkness towards the door, 'let's see if we can open this up.'

Cy pushed his shoulder hard against the stage cupboard door. There were small chinks of light coming through round the outside edge, and through the wood panelling where it didn't fit properly.

'We will never get out,' moaned Aten.

'Yes, we will. The cleaners come in later and we'll just shout for help. But we might not have to wait that long.' Cy started to search in his pockets and then feel about on the floor.

'What are you looking for?' asked Aten.

'The door is fastened with a loop-over catch. If we find a thin piece of wood or something we could slip it through the gap and open it.'

'Something like this?' asked Aten. He held up the stick which went with the triangle. 'I put it in my pocket,' he explained.

By the time they got into the playground it was almost empty. There was no sign of Eddie or Chloe.

'They have my ankh,' Aten said in a worried voice. 'It is not a good thing that people like that should hold my spirit in their hands.'

'I know,' said Cy. 'But it's more likely that they've hidden it somewhere. When they nick things now they never keep them, ever since the last time something went missing and Mrs Chalmers made everybody turn out their pockets. I'll ask Grampa what we should do to get it back.'

It occurred to Cy that he had rather a lot to ask Grampa tonight. He looked around and frowned. Grampa wasn't waiting in his usual spot.

Cy walked slowly back from the school gates and into the playground. There were very few people around now, and none of them was Grampa. He went inside the school and had a quick glance about, and then came out again. He looked up and down the street.

'I don't understand it,' he told Aten. 'He usually comes early so that we can have a chat with Mrs Turner at the crossing.'

'Why don't we ask the cross lady?' suggested Aten.

'Who? Oh, I see,' said Cy. He walked over and called to Mrs Turner who was on the other side of the road. 'Have you seen my Grampa?'

Mrs Turner came over to speak to Cy. 'No, I didn't,' she said. 'But he might have slipped past without me spotting him. It was very busy today.'

'I wonder where he is,' said Cy.

Occasionally Grampa was a few minutes late. But never more than four or five. Cy checked his watch. It was now over twenty minutes since school had finished.

'Here comes Mrs Fortune with the twins,' said Mrs Turner. 'She lives just along the road from your Grampa. We'll ask her.'

Mrs Fortune shook her head. 'No,' she replied, as she reached the little group. 'I didn't see him at all today. He usually passes my house in the morning when he goes for his paper, but I was a bit rushed earlier on. I had to take Paula to the dentist.' She smiled at Cy. 'Maybe your Grampa had an appointment, and you are supposed to meet him somewhere else?'

Cy tried to remember. Had Grampa told him that he wouldn't be at school to pick him up this afternoon? Cy frequently forgot things. If he was asked at home to fetch something, by the time he got to his room he often hadn't a clue what he was looking for. Once he even forgot that he was actually on an errand. He had been sent to get the car keys from upstairs, and been told to run as fast as he could. Everyone was waiting in the driveway, and they were already late for Uncle Jim's wedding. When Cy got to the top of the stairs the spare room door was open so he had gone in. Then he had just sat down, switched on the computer, and started playing a game. His dad and mum had been furious with him. They were always saying that he didn't listen properly, too busy day-dreaming. He did try. Though sometimes the more he tried to concentrate, the worse it became.

Grampa had thought out a strategy for him involving a big old-fashioned brass curtain ring. When the curtain ring was in one of his pockets then Cy knew that there was something he was supposed to do, or something important to remember. If Grampa had changed the school pick-up time or place, then he would have told Cy to put the ring in one of his pockets. Cy searched his clothing. There was no brass ring.

Cy shook his head. 'No,' he told Mrs Fortune and Mrs Turner. 'Grampa didn't say he was going somewhere else.'

'Then he's probably on his way here,' said Mrs Turner reassuringly.

'Why don't you boys walk on?' said Mrs Fortune. 'I'm at number 24. If he's not at home go to my door and wait for me. I've a prescription to collect so I won't be long behind you. Then we'll

phone your mum or dad and find out what's
what.'

'Very likely you'll meet him on the road,' said
Mrs Turner, and she put her hand on Cy's shoulder
as she saw them across.

'You are worried?' asked Aten as the boys began
to walk down the main road together.

'A bit,' admitted Cy. 'It's not like him to be late.
He was in the army for most of his life and he has
a set routine for everything, even eating and
sleeping.'

'My uncle Horemheb is a military man,' said
Aten. 'He is in the army of the Pharaoh. All things
are done by command, including walking and
breathing.' Aten began to strut along in front
swinging his arms and stamping his feet.

Cy laughed. 'Grampa's not quite like that.' But
Cy knew that Grampa did walk very straight with
his head held high. Now Cy had a clear view of the
road all the way down to the traffic lights and
there was no sign of a tall figure with white hair.

It was the same about ten minutes later when
they got to Grampa's street. The long avenue with
trees on either side stretched away before them. It
was empty. Cy opened the little wooden gate into
the neatly kept garden. He led Aten round to the

back of the house and tried the back door.

'It's locked,' said Cy. He stared at the door. 'He hardly ever locks his door.'

'One should always fasten one's door,' said Aten. 'There are many thieves about.'

Cy managed to smile. 'So you too have that problem in Ancient Egypt? Our local police say that "Theft is the scourge of the modern age".' Cy quoted from the crimewatch talk which the community policeman had given his class a few months ago.

Cy tried the door again. 'It feels as though he's got the bolt on. He only does that when he's going to bed. Let's try the front.'

They rang the front door bell, peered through the letter-box, and knocked on the windows.

'It's kind of creepy,' said Cy uneasily. He stood back and gazed at the house. The potted plants stood silently in rows on the window-sills, the curtains hung still. 'I think there's something wrong.'

'Perhaps we could go in there,' said Aten, and pointed to the side of the house. High up on the wall the bathroom window stood open.

'We could never climb up so high,' said Cy.

'I might be able to,' said Aten. 'Look.' Beside the

house grew a birch tree, tall and silvery-smooth it stretched up and up, with the top branches brushing against the roof. 'It is no higher than a palm tree.'

'I don't know,' said Cy doubtfully.

As Cy hesitated Aten scuffed his trainers off, then hugging the tree-trunk loosely with his arms, he placed the soles of his feet flat against the bark. Crouching almost double he scuttled rapidly up the tree, then swung along a branch and clambered in through the bathroom window.

In a few moments Aten had unbolted the back door and the two boys were in the house.

'Grampa,' called Cy, as he went from room to room.

It only took a minute to find him. He was lying just inside his bedroom door, where he had fallen while getting out of bed. One arm was stretched out and one was twisted underneath him.

'Grampa.' Cy's voice was no more than a whisper. He knelt down and touched his Grampa's face. The old man's eyelids flickered.

Aten squatted down beside Cy. 'Tell me where to go to fetch the doctor.'

'Doctor?' Cy's heart was thudding so hard that it was sore in his chest. 'Doctor,' he repeated.

'Yes.' Aten spoke clearly. 'Keep calm and tell me where the doctor lives.'

Cy looked into Aten's brown eyes. His own eyes were going blurry, the way they always did when he was worried, or scared, or stressed. Like when he was trying to do neat writing, or remember something important he had been told. 'Doctor,' he said again. Aten nodded.

Cy knew that there was an emergency number you could telephone, but his brain was refusing to co-operate. He couldn't remember. And any time when he couldn't remember obvious things people just lost patience with him. If it was a classmate they would sneer or laugh at him, and walk away. Adults mostly got angry. Only Mrs Chalmers and Grampa knew just to wait a second or so longer. Cy gave a little sob. How could he forget a simple number? He *mustn't* forget. Grampa's life depended on it. He blinked and stared at Aten.

'Doctor?' Aten said again, very gently. Then he looked directly at Cy, and he smiled.

Cy jumped to his feet. '999,' he said at once. 'Aten, can you put the bedcovers on him and try to keep him warm? I'll phone the emergency services.'

The paramedics and Mrs Fortune with her twins

arrived together. 'I'll phone your parents,' said Mrs Fortune as she watched Grampa being carried out in a stretcher.

'Don't you worry, son,' said one of the ambulance team as he helped Cy into the ambulance. 'Your Grampa looks like a tough old soldier.'

Cy leant across and took Grampa's hand. Faintly, under the pale, papery skin, a pulse kept time with Cy's heart.

Chapter 15

C y was running. Running as fast, and as hard, as he could. But his legs were heavy, his thighs and his ankles weighted down so that he could barely lift his feet to make each step. He knew that he had to keep going. Something urgent, something important to do. Suddenly he stopped. What was it? What was it that he must find? He looked around in the grey fog. All he could see was a small figure dressed in a black cape walking in front of him, marching upwards in the long, dark tunnel. Cy reached

out and touched the person's back.

As the cloak fell away from his shoulders the Dream Master turned round. 'Where's Aten?'

Cy let his hand fall to his side. 'I don't know,' he said. 'He must have got lost.'

'Lost!' shrieked the dwarf. 'Lost! Great Galloping Goddesses! How can you mislay an Ancient Egyptian boy?'

Cy shook his head. 'I don't know. I was . . .' he stopped. What *had* he been doing? How and when had he lost Aten?

'Listen.' The dwarf pushed his face angrily close to Cy's own. 'I have broken two hundred and twenty-two types of rules and regulations to get myself into *your* TimeSpace to collect that boy and replace him in *his* TimeSpace, and when I do . . .' the dwarf drew in a deep breath, '. . . he's gone. Can't you keep your eye on him for a single swithering second?'

'Something happened,' said Cy, 'but I can't remember what it was. And now there's something I've got to do, and I can't remember that either.'

'I'll tell you what you've got to do,' snarled the dwarf. 'Find Aten and help me send him home.'

'He doesn't want to go back,' said Cy.

'He *must* return.'

'Why?'

The Dream Master hesitated. 'Time and fate . . . and, er . . . sequence of events. There could be dreadful historical consequences if he doesn't.'

'Like what?' asked Cy.

'For goodness' sake! I don't know, exactly.'

'Aten is *not* going back into the tomb to die,' declared Cy.

'He has to go back.'

'No,' said Cy.

'Yes,' said the Dream Master.

'*NO!*' Cy shouted. 'NO! NO! NO!' He grabbed the cloak and tried to throw it over the Dream Master's head, but it ended up over his own. The more Cy struggled, the more entangled he became. The dwarf was pulling against him, and he seemed to have grown an extra pair of hands. 'No!' Cy kept yelling as he fought against the darkness.

'It's all right. You're OK.' His dad was beside his bed. 'I've got you, son.' He put his arms around Cy's shoulders and helped him sit upright, free of the duvet covers. 'You're having a bad dream. It's all the worry about Grampa. You're fine now.'

Grampa! Cy leant back on his pillow as it all came flooding back. The ambulance ride to the hospital. Mum and Dad arriving. Hours of wait-ing. Grampa lying in bed, not looking like Grampa. The doctor saying it was a very mild stroke; just to go home now; that Grampa was in the best place. The journey home . . . He must have fallen asleep on top of his bed almost as soon as he lay down.

'Come down to the kitchen,' said Dad. 'Lauren's put the kettle on.'

'Here, Beansprout, have some tea.' Lauren thrust a mug under Cy's nose. 'Hero of the hour according to Mrs Fortune,' she said as she slid a plate of chocolate biscuits across the table. 'Managed to dial 999 and get Grampa to the hospital double-quick.'

Behind Lauren's head Cy's dad winked at him and rolled his eyes madly. Cy smiled as he unwrapped a biscuit.

His mum put her hand on his arm. 'I phoned the hospital again since we came home. They say Grampa's doing fine. And I let Mrs Turner and Mrs Fortune know. Oh,' she added, 'Mrs Fortune said to tell you that Aten said he would be OK. He would find his own way back.'

Later, Cy lay in bed and stared at Luke Skywalker, Han Solo and Princess Leia. Where is

Aten? he asked them silently. The trio stared back. Princess Leia's face showed not a flicker of sympathy. Aten had told Mrs Fortune that he'd find his own way back. And with all the confusion about Grampa no-one asked the question that was now bothering Cy.

Back to where?

Chapter 16

For three days and nights in the Red Land the dust storm blew. Wandering in the great desert, I prayed to Sebek, God of Water, as I huddled close to my camel. Thirty days since the last oasis with no star to show the way. I thought I was lost for ever.' Cy heard Aten's voice before he actually saw him sitting on the front steps of the school the next morning.

'I don't believe this!' Cy marched right into the little group gathered around Aten in the playground. 'What are you doing?' he demanded. 'I

was worried about you. I thought you were lost!'

Aten looked up. 'I was,' he said. He grinned at Cy. 'In fact, I suppose I still am.'

Cy grabbed Aten's arm and dragged him to one side. 'What happened last night? Where did you go?'

'Mrs Fortune kindly gave me food. Then she spoke at the thing you call telephone and said that your mother had told her that Grandfather was safe at the place of the doctors. Then she said it would be dark soon, and did I know where I was staying. I could say truthfully that I did, and I knew it was time to go. So I went.'

'Where?'

'I was very clever,' said Aten proudly. 'I had considered all things carefully. I knew that I might not find my way to your house, so I returned to Grandfather's house. I did not think he would mind. As he was not there, I could guard his property against thieves. I slept on the floor. It was very comfortable. Also,' Aten waved his arms in front of Cy, 'I borrowed some of Grandfather's clothes. They fit better than yours did.'

Cy shook his head. Apart from having a slightly crumpled appearance, Aten didn't look too bad. He had one of Grampa's more modern jumpers over a shirt, and a pair of corduroy trousers which were doubled over at the waist. Cy shoved the pocket linings back inside the trousers, rebuttoned the shirt and explained as best he could the purpose and function of a trouser zip.

'Is your grandfather well?' asked Aten.

'Mum phoned the hospital this morning. They said he was a bit better but hadn't eaten anything yet. She's going to see him later.'

'That is good. You are happier today?'

Cy nodded. 'Yes . . . except I'm worried in case anyone saw you at Grampa's house. They might have phoned the police, and then I'd have to try to explain how you got here.'

'No-one saw me,' said Aten. 'I knew to stay away from the windows in case people thought I was a thief. This morning I ate a strange, lumpy, grey substance from what I hope was a cooking pot. Although this food was more like elephant spoor than camel, it was not unpleasant.'

'Porridge,' said Cy. 'Grampa makes porridge every night for his breakfast the next day.'

'So . . .' Aten smiled at Cy. 'Everything is cool.'

'Yeah, *right*,' said Cy.

'Right on. Actually,' said Aten.

'What?'

'Vicky told me that was a good thing to say.' Aten stuck up his thumb and jabbed it forwards at Cy. He nodded his head several times. 'Right on!'

'I was being sarcastic, *actually*,' said Cy. 'Things are neither cool nor right at this moment. If you remember, certain people,' he stopped for a moment and glanced around the playground, '*certain people* have got your ankh, and I'm not sure how we can get it back.'

Aten raised his hand. 'Do not worry any more. Already this morning I have spoken to Mrs Chalmers. I said that I believed that I had mislaid it. She said that as soon as class starts we shall all have a great ankh hunt.'

But, despite everyone enthusiastically searching, Aten's ankh did not turn up. Cy watched Eddie and Chloe as they happily helped look in drawers and under chairs, and he knew by the expressions on their faces that the amulet was not going to be found in the classroom. The Mean Machines were completely unconcerned as Mrs Chalmers went from desk to desk.

'Perhaps Aten dropped it in the assembly hall during rehearsal yesterday?' suggested Chloe.

Mrs Chalmers stared hard at Chloe's innocent, smiling face. 'I think it would be a *very good thing indeed,*' she said firmly, 'if the ankh turned up before school finished this afternoon. We'll begin lessons now, but perhaps later on some of us could go along to the assembly hall and have a look.'

Aten glanced at Cy. 'The great hall,' he said, 'is where they have hidden it.'

'We'll go there at last bell,' Cy told Aten. 'It's sure to be empty, and we'll have plenty of time to search around.'

124

Chapter 17

Lessons were so boring, thought Cy, as Mrs Chalmers asked the class to take out their workbooks and settle down for a bit. He much preferred *doing* things, although Mrs Chalmers had explained dozens of times that writing things out *was* doing them. She called it 'theoretical' doing.

'We really do need written work, Cy,' she'd say, 'otherwise civilization would be lost, plans would go wrong. People can't remember every detail in their heads.'

Cy watched Aten copying out English words onto the lined paper which Mrs Chalmers had given him. He, too, was having trouble getting his letters to sit neatly in their places.

'It's such a waste of time, isn't it?' said Cy.

Aten looked astonished. 'Oh no!' he said. 'It is extremely tedious and I could find more interesting things to do, but it is not time wasted. Writing is a powerful force. Those who read my words will know what I know, feel what I feel.' He showed his work to Cy.

Cy looked at Aten's squiggly writing. It was even worse than his. 'Er . . . very good,' he said.

'I don't think it is, actually,' said Aten. He put his pencil down. 'There is a better way to practise writing. Do you have any sand?' he asked Mrs Chalmers.

'The janitor brought us some bucketfuls to help with the play,' said Mrs Chalmers. 'Cy will show you where they are.'

Aten filled a shallow plastic tray three-quarters full, then he added some water and smoothed the sand out flat.

'Now, you use your finger . . .' He began to draw some letters. 'See!' He showed Cy. 'It is much clearer. Malik, the chief scribe, teaches all new

126

shapes this way. He says that you learn better because you have to push against the wet sand. Your eye has to pay more attention, and your arm and wrist have to work harder, so they remember more.' Aten stood back and admired his word.

Cy stuck his forefinger deep into the damp sand. He began to carve out his least favourite word to write, *thorough*.

'Slowly,' said Aten over his shoulder, 'push deep and hard so that you feel the shape with your whole body, and follow carefully with your eyes.'

'Oh,' said Cy when he had finished. 'Oh.'

It was the only time he had written *thorough* properly on his first attempt. Usually his *t* or the tail of his *g* were facing in the wrong direction.

'So now,' said Aten, 'the boy scribes practise and practise the same shape over and over again, and, as the sand becomes drier under the hot Egyptian sun, it becomes easier to do. But as it becomes easier to do, so we are more careless, and sometimes Malik is not satisfied with the shape done on the dry sand and he throws water over it and makes us begin again. Only when he is happy are we allowed to write with a stick in the sand, and then eventually to paint with brush and palette.'

Cy picked up his pencil and stuck it in the sand. He began to write again.

'Not so good,' said Aten critically. 'You need to practise lots.' He looked out of the window. 'You are luckier than I,' he said. 'Your sun is not so hot. Here the sand will take longer to dry so you have more time to learn the letter shapes.'

Cy stared long and hard at the sand tray. At home there were some seed trays in the garden hut and an old bag of sand in the garage. Perhaps he could make his own Egyptian letter-learner . . .

Aten clapped Cy on the shoulder and winked. 'You will get better at it,' he whispered. 'And just think. You have only twenty-six to learn. I have seven hundred!'

Cy looked up at Aten. There was something about him that he hadn't noticed before. It was his face. Because of his height he had thought Aten to be a boy of roughly his own age, but Cy realized that he must be a little older. Older and wiser. Wise the way Grampa was wise. The way you become if many different things happen to you.

In the afternoon they all worked on their Egyptian costumes. Some groups were cutting out breast-plates from gold card, while others made jewellery from painted pasta shapes, coloured straws and beads. Mrs Chalmers asked Aten if he would mind sitting still in a chair for twenty minutes so that she could make a plaster cast of his features. She spread Vaseline all over Aten's face while Cy cut pieces from the face-clay bandage roll and soaked them in a bowl of lukewarm water.

'You will make a fine Tutankhamun,' Mrs Chalmers told Aten as she laid the wet strips carefully across his face.

'I will,' said Aten, and he smiled. His forehead and chin had begun to disappear under the layers of gauze strips.

'Don't move!' scolded Mrs Chalmers. She worked quickly, moulding the damp plaster against Aten's features before it could dry. Slowly his face, from ear to ear, and from forehead to chin, was completely covered in white clay.

'I'll leave the underside of your nose free so that you can breathe,' said Mrs Chalmers. She placed the last few strips across Aten's mouth and smoothed them down. Then she stood back. 'Aten,' she said, 'Aten, you look magnificent!' When the plaster was completely dry the rest of the class gathered round as Mrs Chalmers gently eased the mask mould free from Aten's face. She held it up in front of him. 'What do you think?'

Aten reached out and, very slowly, he touched the copy of his features. He frowned and then nodded once or twice. 'Let me see again the decoration that you will place upon it,' he said.

Cy brought the book which had the photograph of Tutankhamun's golden portrait mask.

'It is made of solid gold, decorated with blue glass, lapis lazuli and carnelian,' said Mrs Chalmers.

'With the head-dress of the Vulture Goddess of Upper Egypt and the Serpent Goddess of Lower Egypt,' continued Aten.

'Ah, so that is what the animals represent,' said Mrs Chalmers, looking more closely at the picture. 'How interesting.'

'The Cobra Crown,' murmured Aten.

'It is amazing that it survived,' said Vicky. 'Most tombs were robbed.'

'That is true,' said Aten. 'But then, thieves can always find ways to steal what is not theirs.' He glanced across at Chloe, who blushed and looked away. 'Although,' Aten laughed, 'the watchers of the labyrinth of three thousand rooms at Lake Moeris are never disturbed. These guards are neither men nor dogs, but crocodiles. Large, hungry crocodiles.'

'No way!' said Cy.

'Wrong,' said Aten. 'There is always a way through a labyrinth.'

'"No way" doesn't mean that there is no way,' said Mrs Chalmers. 'It's a modern expression of surprise or, say, disbelief. Like for instance, if you told me that you understood the riddle of the Sphinx, then I might say "No way!"'

'But understanding the Sphinx is not so very hard—' began Aten.

'What Mrs Chalmers means,' Cy interrupted quickly, 'is that saying "No way" is just like saying "Wow" or something.'

'Wow. Or something,' repeated Aten.

'Goodness me!' said Mrs Chalmers, looking at her watch. 'Is that the time? I must hurry to clear up. There is a staff meeting immediately after school tonight.'

Cy and Aten went to the assembly hall as soon as the last bell went.

'The Mean Machines must have put your ankh somewhere in here,' said Cy, looking about. 'They'd be frightened to get caught with it on them.'

'But where?' said Aten. 'The hall is huge.'

131

Cy went across to the stage cupboard and peered inside. 'Someone's been in here again,' he said. 'I'll pull out the pyramid and then we can look among the props.' Just as they managed to manoeuvre the pyramid out into the hall, the door opened and Eddie and Chloe swaggered in.

'Looking for something?' sneered Eddie.

'Yes,' said Cy, in a tired voice, 'and I could catch up with Mrs Chalmers before she goes into the staff meeting and tell her that we haven't found it yet.'

A slightly anxious look passed between Chloe and Eddie.

'All right, camel boy. You can have your silly necklace back.' Chloe ran forward, lifted the top flap of the pyramid, and took Aten's amulet from its hiding place. 'Here! Catch!' she shouted, and she flung the ankh far above her head. The silver surface reflected the light from the long windows as the ankh was hurled high into the air. For a brief moment it hung above their heads, and then it began to fall. Behind the little group the huge cardboard pyramid started to topple forward.

'Look out!' cried Cy. He jumped up and pushed Aten to one side as the great pyramid came down on top of them. It struck them as it fell, sending them all sprawling.

Aten sat up first. He raised his fist in triumph. 'I have it,' he said. He opened his hand to reveal his ankh. And with a happy smile he raised his arms and looped the leather cord of the silver amulet over his head.

As the ankh fell into place round his neck Cy remembered the fear in the Dream Master's voice, the look of terror on his face when Cy had been about to give Aten back his amulet. He spoke aloud to Aten. 'The Dream Master didn't want you to have your ankh back in this time and space.'

Aten shrugged. 'There cannot possibly be any harm in my putting it on. It will help to keep me safe. Wearing it will prevent me from being trapped in the tomb.' He lifted his hand and adjusted the cord round his neck, and as he did so his fingers held the silver amulet.

There was a shuddering crack in the air around him. A bright white light exploded out of the ankh and sent a thousand fractions of colour hurtling into space. And then the fabric of Time tore open and they were sucked inside the spinning, whirling vortex.

Chapter 18

Cy screamed. He was falling. Tumbling down and down, inside the Great Pyramid. He flailed about with both hands as he fell, desperately trying to find something to grab on to. Close beside him he could hear Aten yelling.

'We're going back! We're going back!'

Cy landed on a hard surface. Solid ground below him, and – he felt about cautiously – around him, and . . . above? He couldn't see above.

'Aten?' Cy called. There was a groan and Cy could just make out Aten sprawled alongside him

in the darkness. 'Where are we?' Cy whispered.

'In the tomb,' wailed Aten. 'The worst place I could be.'

'Not the worst,' said Cy, trying to be cheerful. 'I mean there have to be worse places than this.'

'Only one.' Aten shuddered. 'Thank the gods we are not at Lake Moeris with the crocodiles.'

From within the darkness Cy heard a sliding thump.

'What was that?'

'What was what?' asked Aten.

'Didn't you hear anything?' said Cy, and then he dug his nails into Aten's arm as he heard the same noise again. Only this time louder, and closer. 'What *is* that?'

'I can't see,' said Aten. 'We need light, some torches . . .'

Further down the passageway a ruddy glow crept along the wall. Cy scrambled to his feet. 'Come on. Let's go that way.'

'Someone has left flares to show the way,' said Aten. He reached up and lifted a burning torch from its bracket. Behind them came a noise of something heavy slithering across the ground.

Cy glanced back nervously. 'I don't like that noise,' he said. 'I don't know what it is. But I know that I definitely don't like it.' He took down another torch. 'At least we can see a bit better now.'

'If we are in a burial place there should be wall paintings,' said Aten. He held his torch high. 'Ah, yes . . .'

In the dim flickering light they could see pictures on the walls. Figures with kohl-lined eyes, names in elaborate cartouches, and many, many lines of writing.

'Can you read what this says?' Cy asked.

'It tells us of the gods. There is Horus, falcon of the sky, and there is Sebek,' Aten shivered, 'with the head of a crocodile.'

'It must have taken *years* to write it all out,' said Cy. 'I'd hate to have had to do that.'

'To be a scribe is a privilege. It means you have an honoured place in society,' said Aten, 'with much power and wealth. You would pay no taxes.'

'Well, I suppose that is an advantage,' Cy admitted grudgingly. 'If you could earn lots of money then it might be worth it.'

'A scribe's work has much more worth than mere money.' Aten pointed at the hieroglyphs. 'Here upon this wall is written wisdom, and ideas.' He stretched out his fingers and touched Cy gently on the forehead. 'Ideas,' he repeated. 'More valuable than gold or incense. More precious than water in the desert.'

Cy looked again at the picture-writing. He thought of the tremendous effort involved. 'Writing is such a lot of work,' he said.

'Without writing,' said Aten, 'knowledge would be as perfume in the air. Across time and space, with writing, we are able to meet the minds of others.' Cy followed Aten as he moved along, examining the drawings and the script.

'This,' said Aten, 'tells of the Journey to the Afterlife. Anubis weighs the person's heart against the Feather of Truth. See, there are the judges seated on their thrones. They will watch to see on which side the scales come to rest. Insincerity will be found out. A heavy heart is full of deceit and will tip the balance down.'

'Like Chloe and Eddie,' said Cy. 'Pretending to be nice, but nasty on the inside.'

'Chloe and Eddie,' repeated Aten. 'They are as crocodiles. Wide smiles to devour the innocent, but remember, those who deal in darkness will remain in the dark.'

Again Cy heard the strange noise. He looked back down the tunnel. Was there something moving there in the dark, just beyond the light cast by their torches? He shivered. A very vivid imagination, Mrs Chalmers had told his mum and dad on parents' evening. Too vivid. He turned his head firmly to the front and continued walking after Aten. 'Why do you think we are going downhill?'

'Don't all tunnels slope down?' said Aten.

Just as Aten spoke, there was an unexpected dip in the ground beneath them. Aten stumbled and then stopped. Ahead of them were two passageways. Cy peered into the gloom. The passage on the right looked drier, the wall paintings fresher and cleaner. 'Which way?' he asked.

'I don't know,' replied Aten. 'They both look exactly the same.'

'No,' began Cy. 'The one on the right is better . . .' Cy stopped speaking and focused his eyes. He looked from right to left and then back again. The tunnels now appeared identical. 'I thought . . .'

'What?' asked Aten.

'Nothing,' said Cy. 'Let's go on. I don't like this place at all.'

They took the right fork and walked on . . . and on.

'Soon we must reach a hieroglyph which tells us where we are,' said Aten. He held up his torch to

138

illuminate an elegant cartouche. 'This . . .' he began. Then he stopped, and reaching out a trembling finger, he traced the outline of the picto-grams. Cy could see an owl, a plaited tress . . .

'E-M-,' Aten began to spell out the word, 'Emseh.' Aten's voice gurgled in his throat.

'Are you all right?' Cy asked him.

Aten pointed to the hieroglyphs. 'It says . . . it says . . .'

'What?' cried Cy in exasperation. He held his own torch closer. There was a scraping sound, heavy and dull, from near their feet.

'Eeeeeeeeeeeee!' Aten's voice screeched in terror directly into Cy's ear.

'What is it?' Cy looked around wildly and then followed Aten's pointing finger. Just beyond them in the darkness he could make out a low, hulking shape. And then, two pinpricks of dull red. 'What is it?' he repeated. He shook Aten by the arm. 'What is it?'

'Now I understand,' said Aten. 'The tunnels, the noises . . .' His voice stuttered in fear. 'We are in the labyrinth . . . in the labyrinth with the crocodiles.'

Chapter 19

Cy grabbed Aten by the arm and ran. 'You keep to the left in a maze, don't you?'

'I thought that you turned right at each corner,' gasped Aten.

Ahead of them in an opening was a crocodile.

'Omigosh,' said Cy. 'There's two of them. Go the other way!' As he hared up another tunnel behind Aten, Cy tried to think. 'It might be better if we run zigzag,' he yelled. 'I read somewhere it confuses them if you go from side to side.'

'I know the best way to run away from a

crocodile,' Aten yelled back.

'How?'

'Very quickly,' said Aten. 'Egyptian humour,' he added and dodged as Cy tried to punch him.

Cy skidded to halt. 'Let's take a second to think this out,' he said. 'I'm sure it's left.' He remembered when all the family had gone to Hampton Court maze. Lauren had insisted that they turned left at every junction. Although, Cy suddenly recalled, they had been in the maze for *hours* before they had found their way out. 'When we got lost in Hampton Court maze,' said Cy, 'I'm sure Lauren said that the key to getting out was to keep left.'

'Lauren?' said Aten.

'*Lauren!*' yelped Cy, as he caught sight of his sister running along the tunnel.

'Cy, what are you doing here?' Lauren gave her brother a puzzled look. She looked around her. 'What am *I* doing here?'

'Omigollygosh!' said Cy. 'What's going on?'

'I don't know,' said Aten. 'She was not with us in the assembly hall.'

'I was with Baz and Cartwheel,' said Lauren. 'What is this place, anyway?'

'How can she have got here?' asked Cy.

'I know!' cried Aten. 'It is because you

mentioned her. You told me that's what happened in your special dream, and you just said her name a moment ago.'

'But where has she come *from*?' said Cy. 'Where should she be at this moment that she's not?'

'It is very strange,' said Aten. 'Her friends will not know what has happened to her.'

'Hey, what gives?' said a voice from the darkness. 'Isn't this the *weirdest* place?'

'Absolutely.'

Cy whirled round. Baz and Cartwheel were now on either side of Lauren.

'Terrific set for your band, Aten,' said Cartwheel, looking about. She reached out and touched one of the walls. 'These wall paintings are so realistic.'

'That is certainly true,' said Aten. In the distance there was the scrabbling sound of claws. Aten glanced nervously behind them. 'May reality remain an illusion more real than I hope you ever find out.'

'Sorry?' said Lauren.

'Let us pray that close by here there is a swampy underground lake where crocodiles may wish to stay,' said Aten to Cy in a low voice. 'Although, it is said that they are attracted by human voices.'

'This is an *amazing* place,' said Baz. 'Kind of funky.' She looked beyond Aten's head. 'Wow! Those two crocodiles look as if they're actually alive!'

Cy and Aten looked at each other. Then Cy shouted out, 'It's not *me* that's making it happen! It's *you*!'

'No. Way!' said Aten.

'Yes!' yelled Cy. 'Just a second ago you said that crocodiles are attracted by human voices and now they are here! And think back. Since we landed in this place every thought you've had has happened. We fall inside the pyramid, then you think a worse place to be would be in a maze with crocodiles. Next minute we are in a maze. You said we needed light. Zap! Torches appear. To me the tunnels seemed different. You said that you thought they were the same, and I look again, and they were! It's *you*! You're doing it!'

Aten shook his head.

'You *are*!' Cy insisted. 'You mentioned Lauren, and her Boy Band groupie friends, and hey presto!'

'Boy Ba—' repeated Aten.

'No! Don't' – Cy clapped his hand over Aten's mouth – 'say it!' He held up his hand as Aten opened his mouth. 'Don't even think it. Think of something else. Think of *anything* else.'

'My mind keeps coming back to crocodiles,' wailed Aten. He stopped, screamed out loud and put both his hands over his mouth. 'I said it! I said it!' He moaned again and then squeezing his eyes tight, he shouted out, 'A lake, a swampy lake. Crocodiles, please stay in the water.'

There was a splashing sound behind them, and the largest of the crocodiles flapped its tail around in a large, spreading pool of slime.

'That's so *cool*!' said Baz. She took a few steps forward, knelt down, and held out her fingers. 'Isn't he cute?'

'Omigosh,' said Cy.

'Here, boy,' said Baz. 'Come and I'll scratch behind your ears.' The large reptile heaved itself forward. Its huge jaws opened up.

'Think of something,' hissed Cy. 'Fast!'

'What?'

'A muzzle!'

'What's a muzzle?' asked Aten.

'A cage-like thing which locks round its mouth.'

'Like that?'

'Good,' said Cy. 'Now think up another one.'

'Oh, no,' shouted Cy as he saw that the larger

crocodile was now wearing two muzzles. 'One *each.*'

'Sorry,' said Aten.

Being muzzled confused the crocodiles. They began to walk backwards, shaking their heads from side to side.

'Listen!' said Cy. 'Remember at the beginning when you said the crocodiles were a bit like Chloe and Eddie? And . . . and,' Cy's voice rose in excitement, 'you also said that people like that should stay in the dark. So . . .' Cy grabbed the torch from Aten's hand and pulled him further up the tunnel. 'Let's move away and see what happens. I think that the crocodiles will stay in the dark.'

'You don't mean,' said Aten, 'that those crocodiles could actually be Chloe and Eddie?'

Cy nodded. 'Yes . . . No . . .' He shook his head. 'I don't know. Come on,' he said to his sister and her friends. 'We have to move on.' Then he turned to Aten. 'Think of a clear, dry space with some benches to sit on.'

The benches *were* an odd shape, but at least they now had somewhere to rest.

'How is this happening?' asked Aten. 'I have never had dreams like this before.'

'Your ankh.' Cy pointed to Aten's neck.

'Remember I said the Dream Master was terrified that you would touch it? He was right when he thought that it might connect to the Dreamworld. And now everything you think of appears beside you. It's making your imagination come true. A bit like dreaming. Perhaps you should take it off, until we can work out what to do.' Aten lifted his hands to obey. Cy reached out and stopped him. 'You'd better not handle it again. Let me take it,' he said. Cy carefully untied the knot at the back of Aten's neck. Just as he reached round to take the silver amulet Lauren leant over.

'Hey, that's pretty,' she said. 'Can I try it on?' She lifted the amulet and slipped it round her neck. 'D'you think this suits me?' she asked her friends.

'Looks great,' said Baz.

'Absolutely,' said Cartwheel.

Aten spoke very slowly and distinctly. 'Please. Give it back to me.'

Cy held his breath. His sister looked from one to the other.

'Oh, all right,' said Lauren. 'If it's going to upset you.' As she began to undo the leather lace, her hand made contact with the ankh itself. 'Were you practising down here with your band?' she asked.

'No,' said Aten.

'NO!' shrieked Cy.

'But I can hear music,' said Lauren, her fingers still fiddling with the ankh.

'Definitely not,' said Cy. 'Give Aten his ankh back.'

'Are you sure?' Lauren put her head to one side. There was a twang from an acoustic guitar. 'That sound like a track from the new BearBoyz CD.'

'Yes, I'm sure,' Cy said hurriedly. 'Now. GIVE ATEN BACK HIS ANKH!'

'Too late, I think,' said Aten.

Lauren was staring with huge eyes down the tunnel beyond them. 'Do I see what I think I see?'

Declan, lead singer of the BearBoyz, who, Cy noticed, appeared to have both a quiff *and* a fringe, was gyrating along the passageway, crooning into a hand-mike.

'I believe we are now in Lauren's dream,' said Aten.

Cy slumped against the wall.

'My dream?' said Lauren. 'Is this *my* dream?'

'This isn't a dream,' said Cy. 'It's a nightmare.'

"'Cos, if it's my dream,' Lauren went on, 'then I might as well have my wishes come true.' She snapped her fingers. 'Let's have some music,' she said. 'And let's have it LOUD!'

The crash of sound from eight twenty-thousand-watt loudspeakers reverberated round the walls. From deep in the darkness Cy heard one of the crocodiles whimper.

'Now,' said Lauren, 'Declan needs a backing group,' she looked at her two friends, 'and we're *it*!'

The sight of the three girls in day-glo lime-coloured lycra micros with black mini crop tops made Cy move himself. He leapt across and snatched the ankh from Lauren's neck.

Now *he* had it. The Ankh of Aten. In his own hands, with its power released. As Cy clasped it between his palms he felt the charge from it surge inside him. Like a divining rod it tapped into his own psychic energy, and then, enhanced and increased, it soared, multiplying, force upon force. He was all powerful. What he wanted he could get. What he wished for he would have. He could create worlds, his dreams would come true.

'I await your command, master,' said a voice at his elbow.

Cy turned. He wasn't really surprised to see a Jedi knight standing a respectful pace away. Cy blinked several times, closed his eyes tightly for a second or two, and then reopened them one at a time.

Princess Leia handed him his light-sabre. 'Come, Obi-Cy Kenobi. We don't have much time,' she said.

'Time.' Cy repeated the word. The force-beam buzzed in his hand. A flickering white light of pure energy cut through the air. Cy felt the power in him. Now he had it all. He was invincible. But . . . only with the ankh.

Cy looked down at the silver amulet lying in his open palm. He needed the ankh, but it wasn't his.

It belonged to Aten. It was his life force. He *must* give it back.

Slowly Cy's fingers began to close.

Chapter 20

our dreams are your own, Cy,' a voice said quietly.

Cy turned round. Grampa was sitting on the long bench in the tunnel. Cy held up the ankh. 'Do I have to let it go? Lose all my dreams?'

Grampa looked at him seriously. 'You'll never lose your dreams, Cy. No-one can take your dreams away from you. No-one.'

Cy reached out and touched Grampa's hand. 'Thanks, Grampa,' he said. 'I'm glad you're here.' Then he turned to Aten. 'Think hard of the school

assembly hall,' he said, 'and then put your hand on your amulet for a single second.'

There was a rushing roar of white light, and with an enormous ripping noise Cy and Aten fell out through the side of the cardboard pyramid.

'Hey!' shouted a loud voice. 'What are you boys up to?' Cy looked up to see a very annoyed janitor. 'Why are you two still here? The bell went nearly ten minutes ago.'

Cy and Aten scrambled to their feet and explained why they were in the assembly hall. 'Well, now that you've found what you were looking for you can clear off home,' said the janitor.

'Do you think Lauren is all right?' said Cy as they went out into the corridor.

'I think it was *my* dream, and that I ended it, so . . . yes,' said Aten. 'I hope so,' he added.

Cy twisted the cord of the ankh firmly round his wrist. It was safe, for the moment. Now he realized what the Dream Master had been so worried about. Dreams out of control were . . . nightmares.

'What about Chloe and Eddie?' asked Cy. 'They couldn't really have been those two crocodiles, could they?'

Aten gripped Cy's sleeve. Walking ahead of them towards the front door were two bedraggled figures. Mud and slime clung to their legs and shoes.

Suddenly the staff room door opened and the teachers came out to go to their staff meeting. Miss Fullbright caught sight of Eddie and Chloe.

'You two have obviously been down at the river,' she said in a stern voice.

'No,' said Chloe.

'Then if you weren't by the river, where did all this pondweed come from?'

'We were in the assembly hall, Miss Fullbright.'

'Yes,' Eddie chimed in. 'We were with Cy and Aten.'

Miss Fullbright turned round. Aten opened his mouth. Cy's heart shook.

'Only these two boys were in the assembly hall,' said the janitor, who had followed them along the corridor. 'Said Mrs Chalmers had given them permission to look for something they'd lost.'

'Yes, that's right,' said Mrs Chalmers. 'Did you find the ankh?'

Cy held up his wrist.

'So, what have you two got to say for yourselves?' Miss Fullbright fixed her eyes back on Eddie and Chloe.

'But we *were* in the assembly hall!' shrieked

Chloe. 'That's how Cy got the ankh back. Because I showed him where we hid it . . . I mean . . . I . . .' her voice tailed off.

Mrs Chalmers raised her eyebrows and folded her arms.

'Don't lie,' snapped Miss Fullbright. 'Lying only makes things worse. There are written warnings everywhere about this, and all school pupils have been told many times that they must *not* go near the river. It is *extremely* dangerous, and if you older children persist in doing it then the little ones will copy you.' She glared at them fiercely. 'Report to me first thing tomorrow morning. I will think of a suitable and severe punishment for you.'

At the patrol crossing Cy and Aten saw Eddie and Chloe limping across the road. Chloe's face was white, and Eddie's legs were shaking so much that he could hardly stand up. There were tendrils of green slime still trailing from their shoes. Eddie's mum was giving him a row. 'Look at the state of you! You've been mucking about by the river-bank, haven't you?'

'I . . . I . . .' stuttered Eddie.

'That is *so* dangerous, Eddie. I hope the school finds out and punishes you for it.'

Chloe's mum was standing well away from her. 'Chloe, dear, you pong something *awful*. We can't possibly go and buy those new shoes you wanted. You'll have to walk a good bit behind me on the way home.'

'What happened to those two?' asked Mrs Turner.

Cy and Aten exchanged glances.

Aten shrugged. 'Yo?' he said.

Cy's dad was waiting to pick him up. 'Would Aten like to come home with you for dinner?'

Aten nodded quickly. 'I would be honoured.'

'We'll have to let your parents know.'

'He can telephone from our house,' Cy said at once.

When they got home Cy made a pretence of telephoning while his father prepared the dinner. Aten watched him in the kitchen.

'In your forward time, men cook,' he said. 'That is very unusual.'

'You're telling me,' said Cy.

'Yes, I am,' said Aten. 'In fact,' he gave Cy a puzzled look, 'I just did.'

They hadn't long to wait before Lauren came rocketing through the door. She scraped back a chair and sat down at the table. 'Wait 'til I tell you this. At last break, Baz and Cartwheel and I, we were lying out just beside the playing-fields in the sun and we fell asleep.'

'Obviously the teachers are working you far too hard at school,' said Cy's dad, plonking a dish of meatballs onto the table. He pointed at it. 'Eat,' he commanded, 'and no whingeing to your mother about my cooking when she gets back from the hospital.'

Aten watched carefully, copying Lauren as she spooned food onto her plate.

'And,' Lauren went on, 'and then I had a really strange dream. We were in this Egyptian tomb, and Aten was there too.'

'How interesting,' said Aten, not looking at Cy. 'Was I doing anything in particular?'

'It was a bit odd. You seemed to have two pet crocodiles.' Lauren took some bread. 'You were with him, Cy.'

Aten picked up a piece of bread. 'And also the BearBoyz.'

Cy choked on his food.

'How did you guess?' said Lauren. 'They *were* there too. And Baz and Cartwheel and I, we were the backing singers.'

'In your dreams!' said Cy.

'Well, *exactly*,' said Lauren. 'But the weirdest thing about the whole thing is that Baz and Cartwheel had the very *same* dream!'

'No. Way!' said Aten.

'Absolutely, no way,' agreed Cy. 'People do *not* have the same dreams. Not exactly the same.'

'Well, there were differences,' admitted Lauren. 'In my dream I was the one standing right next to Declan, whereas Baz says she dreamt it was her.'

'No, it was definitely you,' said Aten.

'What?' Lauren stopped with her glass halfway to her mouth.

'It was you,' said Aten, not noticing Cy's widely swinging foot trying to connect with his leg.

'How do you know?' asked Lauren.

'It's a joke,' said Cy. 'Obviously, it's a joke. Aten's only winding you up. He doesn't even know who Declan is.'

'Yes, I do,' said Aten. 'He's the one with the quiff. Although I prefer it when his hair falls over his eyes.'

'So do I!' said Lauren. 'You have such style, Aten. I spotted that the minute I saw you.'

'And you are so beautiful,' replied Aten.

Lauren blushed.

I don't believe this, thought Cy. He is actually chatting her up. And she's taking it on. My sister and my friend.

'I would like to call you Lauren-Nofret,' Aten went on. 'In my language *nofret* means "beautiful lady". So Lauren-Nofret would be Lauren the lovely.'

'You *are* joking,' Cy told Aten firmly.

'No, truly,' Aten turned to Cy. 'That is why there are Egyptian names like Nefertiti and Nefertari. *Nefer* is similar to *nofret*; it means "good and beautiful".'

'I meant about the *dream*,' said Cy in exasperation, and, as he spoke, he managed to kick Aten under the table.

'Owww!' Aten cried out. He rubbed his ankle. 'It would appear that I am joking.' He smiled at Lauren. 'About the dream,' he added. 'Not about the name.'

'Oh, that's OK,' said Lauren. She looked at him from under her lashes and then she picked up her fork. 'Well, anyway. The dream kind of stopped, and we all woke up. But it was a great experience. So lifelike. I thought it was actually happening.'

Aten, too, picked up his fork. 'Dreams are mysterious things,' he said. He looked down at his food. 'More animal spoor?' he enquired.

'Don't you like meatballs?' Cy's dad asked him.

Aten speared a meatball carefully on the end of his fork. He shut his eyes and put it into his mouth. 'The taste,' he said, 'is not unpleasant.' Under his breath he added, 'Definitely rabbit's.'

They were washing up when Cy's mum came back from hospital visiting.

'Oh, Grampa is *so* much better,' she said, as she flopped into an armchair. Cy's dad went to fetch her some tea. 'You know, Cy, Grampa told me a funny thing happened today. He had been feeling quite poorly, and then he fell asleep in the afternoon and had a strange dream. He was lost in this long dark tunnel, and thought he would never find his way out. Suddenly you came and sat beside him. You took his hand and he knew then that he would be all right. The nurses told me that when he woke up he was smiling, and he ate all of his dinner. They say he is well on the way to recovery now. You can go and visit him tomorrow.'

'So, perhaps there was a purpose to our journey in the labyrinth,' said Aten later as he and Cy walked slowly back to Grampa's house. 'If you had not been there, Grandfather might have remained lost.'

'I thought he was there to help *me*,' said Cy.

Aten shrugged. 'Perhaps both. Who knows? What I *do* know, however, is this.' He stopped walking and turned to face Cy. 'I must go back. Back to the tomb.'

Chapter 21

There was a long, long, silence. Then, 'Why?' asked Cy. His voice came out strange and croaky when he spoke. He looked into the face of his friend, and knew that Aten was not going to change his mind. Cy felt desolate, and also very afraid. 'Why?' he asked again.

'It is hard to explain,' said Aten, 'but I will try.' He waited a moment or two and then with a great sigh, he said, 'I do not belong here. I like it very much. All is wonderful and full of excitement, but . . . it is not my place. I am from somewhere else,

some other space, some other time. I do not understand completely. Half is hidden from me. But this I know, I must return and find my own way.'

'Even to the tomb?' Cy's voice was barely a whisper.

Aten nodded calmly.

'When?'

'I think after your play, which is . . .?'

'Friday,' said Cy. 'The day after tomorrow.'

'So be it.'

In school the following day Aten watched fascinated as Mrs Chalmers made and decorated the elaborate Pharaonic head-dress. She painted the plaster face burnished gold, and carefully outlined the eyes and eyebrows with black kohl. Then she placed the head-dress round it and sealed them together.

'What's your verdict then, Aten?' she asked.

Aten nodded once or twice. 'It is fitting,' he said.

At lunch-time the boys shared sandwiches in the classroom. 'How will you explain my leaving?' Aten asked Cy.

'My mum teaches foreign languages and she sometimes helps to arrange pupil exchanges so I'll tell Mrs Chalmers you've been placed now,' said

Cy. 'The long summer holidays start soon, then I go to secondary school. Let's hope they never get to discuss it properly.'

'And Lauren?'

'Oh, she's nuts about you. She'll believe anything now.'

'Nuts,' repeated Aten. 'Which kind?'

'It's just an expression. Forget it,' said Cy.

'Now we must hurry,' said Aten. 'Lunch-time is nearly over and we have not yet dropped any of our papers outside.'

'Oh yeah, I nearly forgot,' said Cy.

He looked through the classroom window at the two figures trailing round the playground behind the school janitor. Eddie and Chloe had been ordered by the Head to pick up all the litter during every single break until the end of term. This morning Cy had overheard the drama teacher, looking at the sea of orange peel, crisp-bags, sweet-papers, and other rubbish, saying to Mrs Chalmers, 'The playground suddenly seems to have got so messy.'

Mrs Chalmers had replied, with some satisfaction in her voice. 'Well, those two *have* annoyed rather a lot of people over the last months.'

Cy went out into the playground with his

biscuit wrappers, whistling, 'Never smile at a crocodile'.

On Friday afternoon they performed the Procession of the Pharaoh in front of the rest of the school. Mrs Chalmers moved Aten from playing the triangle to being an Egyptian soldier. She said he looked more authentic than anyone else. She gave Cy the triangle and stick. He was sure he struck it at all the wrong places but no-one seemed to notice, and the infant classes adored Aten who strutted about threatening them with his spear. Afterwards Cy asked Mrs Chalmers if he could borrow the small top piece of the pyramid which Innes, Basra and Vicky had made.

'I'll be very careful with it,' he promised.

'I know you will, Cy,' said Mrs Chalmers.

'Oh, and Miss, this is Aten's last day. He goes off at the weekend.'

Mrs Chalmers shook Aten's hand. 'It has been *very* interesting having you in class this week,' she said. 'I hope some of what you saw will be of value to you.'

Aten smiled. 'You are a wise and kind teacher. I have learnt immeasurable amounts.'

*

On Saturday afternoon, while the rest of the family were shopping, Cy laid out the cardboard pyramid on his bed.

'I thought if we sat on either side, and then I let the light from the window shine through the ankh . . .' Cy tailed off. 'Well, it's the best I could think of.'

Aten took his pleated linen kilt from Cy's cupboard and put it on. He combed and oiled his sleek, glossy, black hair, and then draped a thin strip of linen diagonally across his chest.

'I am ready,' he said.

Chapter 22

From the corner of Cy's room the Dream Master stepped forward, and taking the ankh from Cy's wrist, he placed it round Aten's neck.

'I thought you weren't going to do that until Aten had returned to his own time,' said Cy.

'Indeed,' said the Dream Master. He turned and his cloak spun out behind him.

Cy blinked. The walls of the pyramid were no longer cardboard brown, they had become fawn. Cy reached out his hand and touched the sides. It was solid.

'Ah,' he said. He turned. There were the statues, the furniture, the paintings, and the mummy case in the corner.

Aten looked round him. 'We are as we were,' he stated in a flat voice. 'I had hoped——'

'That we would come back at a different bit,' Cy finished for him.

Aten nodded. 'Just a little bit earlier so that I could avoid being captured. But,' he sighed, 'here we are. As before.'

'Mmm, not quite as before,' said Cy. 'It said in one of my books that, as well as the official entrance, there were sometimes secret passages leading from the tombs.'

'But if these passages are secret, how do we find them?' Aten asked him.

'I spoke to Grampa when I visited him at the hospital,' said Cy, 'and he said that we might need a magnetic compass, some chalk, and a ball of string.'

'I do not have these things,' said Aten.

Cy stuck his hands in his pockets, 'But I do,' he said. 'Grampa also said to look carefully at the paintings with the darkest colours where there might be a hidden opening.'

The torch beam was flickering yellow when

eventually Cy heard Aten shout out. Aten pointed to the lower part of the wall where he was searching. 'Look, here! There is a gap in the wall.'

Cy shone the torch into the cavity. A long narrow passage curved away and upwards. Cy peered inside. 'It hardly looks big enough for a person to crawl along,' he said.

'I do not think it was meant to take a person's body,' said Aten.

'Then what?' asked Cy.

'The soul,' said Aten. 'I've heard it said that in the pyramids at Giza there are such passageways to enable the dead Pharaoh's soul to travel freely.'

'To where?' asked Cy.

'These passageways point to the stars,' said Aten. 'To Osiris, and the brightest star in the sky . . .' Aten stopped, and gave Cy a strange look.

'The brightest star in the sky is Sirius,' said Cy.

'Yes,' said Aten. 'Your own name. Cyrus.'

Cy opened his mouth and then closed it again.

'You *were* sent to lead me to safety.' Aten smiled at Cy.

Cy shook his head slowly. 'If what you say is true then this passageway should lead to the outside.' He shone the torch inside again. 'It is *very* narrow. Are you absolutely sure?'

'We are not so large,' said Aten, 'and I will happily follow you.'

Cy groaned. 'I thought you might say that.'

Some time later Cy and Aten struggled out of a narrow opening behind a rocky outcrop high in the Valley of the Kings. Below them, wide and slow, moved the waters of the Nile.

'Look!' cried Aten. 'Tying up by that jetty. There is a royal barge!' He turned to Cy. 'I must go.'

Cy looked at his friend for a long moment. 'You're still wearing my trainers,' he said eventually.

Aten removed one shoe and gave it to Cy. 'I keep the left sandal, as a bond between us,' he said. 'You hold the right one, my friend through Time. I will remember you always, as you remember me.' He struck his brow with his hand and then touched Cy's forehead with his fingertips. 'It is done,' he said.

Cy watched Aten run down the slope towards the great river. This would have to happen Aten's way, and he, Cy, would have to accept what fate dictated.

Suddenly he was aware of a presence beside him. The Dream Master was biting his beard and muttering like a bad-tempered child.

'This is a Right Royal Rameses, I can tell you. Thirteen Thundering Thunderclaps say it's never going to work out. Camels and crocodiles ... of all the Desperate Dynasties, I do not know ...' Cy realized that the little man was as worried as he was.

'He'll be all right,' Cy said.

The barge had moored by the edge of the river. From it came armed soldiers, attendants and white-robed priests. Leading the procession was a young woman, who cried at once in delight as she saw Aten.

'I knew we would find him if we kept looking,' she shouted. 'I knew it.'

'Hesen!' Aten called out her name.

She ran forward and knelt in the sand before Aten. 'General Horemheb has returned and taken control of the army once more,' she said. 'He freed your uncle Ay so that he could search for you.'

'Come forward, Ay,' Aten called out.

An old man stepped from among the officials. 'It is well that you have been found and are safe,' said Ay. Then he turned and stared at the court officials who moved backwards from him. 'Be it known to all, that from this day if any harm comes to Aten, I will be mightily displeased.'

The Dream Master touched Cy's sleeve. 'Aten is safe now. We may go. Take firm hold of my cloak and do not release it.'

Cy reached out and gripped a corner of the black silk. Again he felt the rushing silky wind. But, as Cy tightened his grip, the Dream Master's cloak tore in his hand. Cy gasped. The Dream Master's cloak had ripped and they were separated. The fabric of Time had split, and now he was lost. He was falling, out of sequence, out of place.

With a thump he tumbled onto his own bed. Dazed, Cy sat up and uncurled his fist. In his fingers lay a tiny fragment of the Dream Master's cloak. The piece of black material fluttered and then was still. Cy looked around his room. He knew that he must put it away. Somewhere safe. Under the bottom drawer of his chest of drawers was where he kept his most secret things, away from Lauren's prying eyes: Grampa's war medal, his fossil stone, the matchbox with the sand inside. Cy pulled out the drawer. The fragment of black silky material rippled, and a faint exotic scent brushed his nostrils. Cy hesitated, his fingers curled. A thin tremor lingered in the air. Cy let go, then straightened up and lifted the drawer back in place.

*

A few days later, in school, they were clearing up the classroom before the start of the summer holidays. Vicky and Cy were gathering all the Egyptian display material together. A very subdued Eddie and Chloe were folding up the costumes.

'Put all of that in a box and store it with the props,' said Mrs Chalmers. 'It will be useful when the next Egyptian project is being done.'

As Cy collected the papyrus signs, Vicky stopped to read from one of the display cards, which showed the boy Pharaoh sitting on his throne. 'Why is it,' she asked Mrs Chalmers, 'that here the boy Pharaoh Tutankhamun's name is written as Tutankhaten?'

'Because Tutankhamun changed his name,' said Mrs Chalmers. 'He was originally called Tutankhaten. Not long after he became Pharaoh he changed his name from Tutankhaten to Tutankhamun.'

Cy stopped what he was doing and took the card from Vicky. The name leapt out at him. Tut-Ankh-Aten.

'Aten!' Cy whispered softly. Around him, Time slowed down. Cy looked at the picture. It was a scene from the back of Tutankhamun's throne. His

171

wife was standing before him anointing his chest with perfumed oil. His wife, Ankhesenamen ... Ankh-Hesen-Amen. On her right foot she wore a sandal, the other was bare.

The king sat on his throne. His left foot was sandalled, the other one unshod.

Underneath, it said that no-one knew for certain, but it was believed that this was a sign of great affection between two people. Cy smiled. He knew for certain. 'I am Aten of the Ankh.' That was what Aten had said when Cy had first met him face to face in his dream.

'Tut-Ankh-Aten,' Cy whispered, 'Tut-Ankh-Amun ... Tutankhamun.'

Cy walked over to where the golden portrait mask lay on Mrs Chalmers desk. He remembered Aten's fascination with it, and how it was that after seeing it, Aten had insisted he must return to his own place. Cy lifted the golden mask of the boy king which Aten had posed for. His head spun as he tried to work it out.

Was it this mask which Aten had seen in a class-room in Britain in the twenty-first century and copied for his own sarcophagus? And therefore, if Cy's dream had not flipped over, bringing Aten into Mrs Chalmers' classroom, the explorer

Howard Carter would not have had any mask to find? Or had Aten recognized the face depicted on the gold portrait mask as his own, and that was why he was so insistent about returning? Knowing he had to keep faith with his own destiny.

It wasn't possible. Was it?

Cy traced the outline of Aten's features on the golden mask. That was why it was so similar to the photographs of the original in the Cairo Museum. It *was* the original, or, rather, *more* original than the original.

'Bring peace to your kingdom, Aten,' he said softly. 'Rule wisely and well.'

Cy turned and looked into the mirror which hung on the classroom door. Mrs Chalmers had told him that the Ancient Egyptian word for 'mirror' was *ankh*. Cy raised the golden mask of Tutankhamun to cover his face and stared through the eye-slits at the reflection of the boy Pharaoh. His own eyes gazed back at him. And then, to Cy's astonishment, one eyelid closed slowly in a deliberate wink.

CLOCKWORK
or
ALL WOUND UP
by Philip Pullman

Tick, tock, tick, tock! Some stories are like that.
Once you've wound them up, nothing will stop
them...

A tormented apprentice clock-maker – and a
deadly knight in armour. A mechanical prince –
and the sinister Dr Kalmenius, who some say is
the devil... Wind up these characters, fit them into
a story on a cold winter's evening, with the snow
swirling down, and suddenly life and the story
begin to merge in a peculiarly macabre – and
unstoppable – way.

Almost like clockwork...

'Exciting, scary, romantic and deliciously
readable'
Guardian

SILVER MEDAL WINNER, SMARTIES
AWARD IN 1997

SHORTLISTED FOR THE CARNEGIE
MEDAL IN 1997

ISBN 0 440 86343 0

GHOST ON THE LOOSE
by Helen Dunwoodie

*As she climbed towards the half-landing, Rowan
found herself mysteriously compelled to slow down.
What was so special about Robert's room that he
wouldn't allow anyone else inside it?*

For Rowan it is bad enough having to live with
Robert, Mum's boring new boyfriend, without his
ridiculous obsession with his study. What can he be
hiding there that is so important? Or so horrible?

Rowan's not the only one who's intrigued by the
study. In fact, there's someone who's discovered
Robert's secret and is determined to expose him.
The only problem is that Lady Maisie McNeil is a
ghost and she can't wreak her revenge without a
bit of help from someone in the twentieth century.
It looks like she's found just the girl . . .

ISBN 0 440 86380 5